Step into the world of NYC Angels

Looking out over Central Park,
the Angel Mendez Children's Hospital,
affectionately known as Angel's,
is famed throughout America for being at the
forefront of paediatric medicine, with talented
staff who always go that extra mile for their
little patients. Their lives are full of highs,
lows, drama and emotion.

In the city that never sleeps, the life-saving
docs at Angel's Hospital work hard, play hard
and love even harder. There's *always* time for
some sizzling after-hours romance...

And striding the halls of the hospital,
leaving a sea of fluttering hearts behind him,
is the dangerously charismatic new head of
neurosurgery Alejandro Rodriguez. But there's
one woman, paediatrician Layla Woods, who's
left an indelible mark on his no-go-area heart.
Expect their reunion to be explosive!

NYC Angels

*Children's doctors who work hard and love
even harder...in the city that never sleeps!*

Dear Reader

There are times when we all struggle with issues of self-esteem and self-worth. Sometimes those struggles are based on our own perceptions, but other times the damage is caused by people who come into our lives—people in whom we place our trust. The heroine of NYC ANGELS: FLIRTING WITH DANGER has fled just such a situation. As she faces an uncertain future she must painstakingly sift through what is real and what is not—and she must come to terms with the fact that she is worthy of love. Worthy of true intimacy.

Thank you for joining Brad and Chloe as they face the heartbreak of broken dreams and somehow find the courage to love again. I hope you enjoy reading about their journey as much as I enjoyed writing it!

Much love

Tina Beckett

NYC ANGELS: FLIRTING WITH DANGER

BY
TINA BECKETT

To my dear husband, who has held my hand when I needed it
held and has smiled at my insanely ridiculous desire
to own a chicken, and who promised that some day
I would have one. I'm holding you to that promise, honey!

© Harlequin Books S.A. 2013

Special thanks and acknowledgement are given to Tina Beckett
for her contribution to the *NYC Angels* series

ISBN: 978 0 263 23359 9

Harlequin (UK) policy is to use papers that are natural, renewable
and recyclable products and made from wood grown in sustainable
forests. The logging and manufacturing process conform to the
legal environmental regulations of the country of origin.

Printed and bound in Great Britain
by CPI Antony Rowe, Chippenham, Wiltshire

Born to a family that was always on the move, **Tina Beckett** learned to pack a suitcase almost before she knew how to tie her shoes. Fortunately she met a man who also loved to travel, and she snapped him right up. Married for over twenty years, Tina has three wonderful children and has lived in gorgeous places such as Portugal and Brazil.

Living where English reading material is difficult to find has its drawbacks, however. Tina had to come up with creative ways to satisfy her love for romance novels, so she picked up her pen and tried writing one. After her tenth book she realised she was hooked. She was officially a writer.

A three-times Golden Heart finalist, and fluent in Portuguese, Tina now divides her time between the United States and Brazil. She loves to use exotic locales as the backdrop for many of her stories. When she's not writing you can find her either on horseback or soldering stained-glass panels for her home.

Tina loves to hear from readers. You can contact her through her website or 'friend' her on Facebook.

Recent titles by the same author:

ONE NIGHT THAT CHANGED EVERYTHING
THE MAN WHO WOULDN'T MARRY
DOCTOR'S MILE-HIGH FLING
DOCTOR'S GUIDE TO DATING IN THE JUNGLE

These books are also available in eBook format from www.millsandboon.co.uk

NYC Angels

*Children's doctors who work hard and love even harder...
in the city that never sleeps!*

Step into the world of NYC Angels and enjoy two new stories a month

In March New York's most notoriously sinful bachelor Jack Carter
found a woman he wanted to spend more than just one night with in:
NYC ANGELS: REDEEMING THE PLAYBOY
by Carol Marinelli

And reluctant socialite Eleanor Aston made the gossip headlines
when the paparazzi discovered her baby bombshell:
NYC ANGELS: HEIRESS'S BABY SCANDAL
by Janice Lynn

In April cheery physiotherapist Molly Shriver melted the icy barricades
around hotshot surgeon Dan Morris's damaged heart in:
NYC ANGELS: UNMASKING DR SERIOUS
by Laura Iding

And Lucy Edwards was finally tempted to let neurosurgeon
Ryan O'Doherty in. But their fragile relationship
had to survive her most difficult revelation yet...
NYC ANGELS: THE WALLFLOWER'S SECRET
by Susan Carlisle

Now, in May, newly single (and strictly off-limits!)
Chloe Jenkins makes it very difficult for drop-dead-gorgeous
Brad Davis to resist temptation...!
NYC ANGELS: FLIRTING WITH DANGER
by Tina Beckett

And after meeting single dad Lewis Jackson, tough-cookie Head Nurse
Scarlet Miller wonders if she's finally met her match...
NYC ANGELS: TEMPTING NURSE SCARLET
by Wendy S. Marcus

Finally join us in June, when bubbly new nurse Polly Seymour
is the ray of sunshine brooding doc Johnny Griffin needs in:
NYC ANGELS: MAKING THE SURGEON SMILE
by Lynne Marshall

And Alex Rodriguez and Layla Woods come back into each other's
orbit, trying to fool the buzzing hospital grapevine that the spark
between them has died. But can they convince each other?
NYC ANGELS: AN EXPLOSIVE REUNION
by Alison Roberts

**Be captivated by NYC Angels in this new eight-book continuity
from Mills & Boon® Medical Romance™**

**These books are also available in eBook format
from www.millsandboon.co.uk**

CHAPTER ONE

NOTHING COULD CONCEAL her shame.

Not this time. Still, Chloe Jenkins yanked the belt of her beige trench coat tighter, until she was sure it would cut her in two—much like her heart had been. What had seemed sexy a half-hour ago now seemed unbearably pathetic and sleazy. The New York City subway station was jammed with bodies, even at this hour, and she shoved wet hanks of hair from her eyes, glad to finally be out of the rain.

What was she supposed to do now?

Hurling your wedding rings at your cheating bastard of a husband with the words "Consider this our divorce!" may have seemed like the perfect exit line—the only way to escape with a shred of dignity—but charging out of that hotel room had left her with few options. She was in a huge city where she knew no one.

Except...

The air shuddered from her lungs. There had to be some other way.

She could always go home to Connecticut.

And face her brother? Her family? They'd known the truth all along, but she'd been too much of a naïve sap to listen.

The doors opened and she stepped into the train, careful to keep her bare toes far from the nearest occupant.

She could head to a car rental facility. She had her purse and her wallet, thank heavens.

But she'd foolishly left her shoes behind in the room, and it was illegal to drive like this, even if they'd lease her a car. And if the tie on her coat came loose, she'd be totally exposed.

Her face burned hotter. Okay, maybe she wouldn't be totally exposed, but the peek-a-boo black negligee and sheer panties left little to the imagination.

Even for her ex, who—when she emerged from beneath the cocoon of covers, fury spilling from every pore—had allowed his eyes to crawl over her body, a spark of interest finally coming to life in the drunken depths.

God. Why had she even bothered to try?

Because she didn't believe in giving up. At least, she hadn't before now.

The train suddenly slowed as it came to its next stop, and she lost her balance for a few frightening seconds, scrabbling to regain her handhold while keeping her coat from coming open.

Someone bumped into her from behind as they tried to exit, the hard shove sending her reeling a second time. She bit her lip and tasted blood.

"Sorry." Hands came out to steady her, but Chloe flinched away, terrified someone would find out what she'd tried to do. She checked with the tip of her tongue the damage her teeth had caused. Not exactly the way she'd planned to spend the night.

You're right, baby, she does *look frigid.*

Travis's current paramour had clung to his arm and giggled at the sight of Chloe under the covers, the duvet pulled up to her chin.

What had been meant as a last-ditch effort to save her marriage had turned into a guillotine instead, one that had nicked her, even as she'd released the cord and let it drop—cleaving what had been one into two and setting her free.

Travis hadn't even blinked in the face of her rage. Probably too full of whiskey to care. He'd suggested she stick around…

implied she might even want to join in the fun. Her fist had balled up tight, ready to deliver the mean right hook her brother had once taught her, before she stopped herself, realizing it would do no good.

It was over.

A wave of nausea washed up her throat.

She could call her brother and...do what exactly? It was almost midnight, and Jason was a couple of hundred miles away. Besides, he'd ask all kinds of questions. Was she really ready to publicly admit that Travis had wanted the family's money? He certainly hadn't wanted her. Not really. No matter how charming he'd been during their courtship. No, he'd wanted a leg up in the financial investment industry, which he'd gotten...and more.

God. She'd saved herself for him. And for what? Love sure hadn't been any sweeter on the other side of the marriage bed.

She tried to think.

If she called Jason right now, he was liable to go all big-brotherly on her. She didn't need defending. She needed to get away. For a while, anyway. To plan her next move—at least the one beyond filing for an actual divorce, which she planned to do first thing Monday morning.

So, until then she could just get a room at another hotel.

In her nightgown? Strains of "Pretty Woman" began playing in her head. Yeah. She knew exactly what they'd think she was with plastered hair, thigh-high coat, and no shoes. No respectable hotel would let her through the doors.

And the unrespectable ones...

That was no better solution than the first option. Her eyes went to the tangled colors on the map posted above the doors of the subway train.

As much as she hated the idea, her thoughts circled back to the one person she knew in New York: Brad Davis. She knew where he worked—the Angel Mendez Children's Hospital—

but she had no idea what part of town that was in, or where her brother's old friend lived. Or even what subway line she should be on right now. She knew how to find Brad, though. Social media was good for at least one thing.

Bracing her feet against the sway of the train and digging out her smartphone, she took a deep breath and pulled up her friends list.

Brad paced the living room of his high-rise apartment, half irritated, half intrigued. It was Friday night, and he'd just sent his date home with a smiled apology and a smoothly worded explanation about family coming into town unexpectedly.

Which wasn't a total lie. Chloe *was* practically family. In fact, he'd spent more of his teenage years at Chloe and Jason's house than he had at his own. And despite being known more for his biker jacket, spiked wrist cuff and well-practiced sneer than for his social graces, his best friend's folks had made it clear he was welcome any time. Had made sure he'd known they cared about him, even as he'd wondered if his own parents knew he existed.

And Chloe…

His mind sifted through images of the past, each overlapping the other until it formed a collage of memories, full of pink cheeks and adolescent banter.

No one had been more shocked than he, six years ago, to learn she was getting married, or to arrive at the wedding and realize what a gorgeous young woman she'd grown up to be. Asking her to dance had been the ultimate mistake. As they'd taken one quick spin around the dance floor, the hem of her lacy white gown swishing in time with their slow movements, he'd suddenly realized she was no longer the gawky kid who had tagged along after him and her brother. The glint of a hairpin imprisoning a long graceful curl had made his palms itch. What would happen if he reached up and…

His arms had instinctively tightened to resist the temptation, the act pulling her fully against him. His body had reacted, his pulse rate climbing dangerously. A soft gasp had left her throat, and the fingers that had been politely resting on his shoulder curled into the fabric of his suit jacket.

He'd looked down just as her eyes came up. Raw awareness had shimmered between them, and her teeth had sunk deep into her bottom lip—the lip he hadn't been able to stop staring at. The world around him had faded away, and the self-destructive tendencies he'd thought long gone had swooped down, nearly consuming him.

As if recognizing danger, Chloe's husband had suddenly appeared beside them, his hand outstretched, a warning frown between his brows. He'd spirited her away, a mysterious ethereal creature with huge blue eyes and slender curves. The memory of her body pressed to his had stayed with him long into the night.

Nope. No thinking about curves, racing pulses or anything else. She was his best friend's sister. Sweet. Innocent.

Married.

Nothing like the women he dated—sophisticated women who knew exactly what the words "no strings" meant and would play by his set of rules. Women who were the opposite of Chloe Jenkins.

So what was she doing, wandering the streets of New York at midnight? By herself? She'd said there'd been a hitch in her hotel reservations. Why not just choose another place, then? Or drive home to Connecticut, if it came down to it?

He'd only seen her once since her wedding day, and she'd never attempted to contact him. Until tonight.

He should have said no. Should have reminded himself of that crazy dance and told her to steer clear of him—or told her he had company, with just enough emphasis to let her know exactly what that meant.

But there'd been something about her voice on the phone. A

shaky uncertainty, as if she'd *expected* him to flat-out refuse to let her come up—something he would never do to Chloe, even if Jason weren't his best friend. Even if seeing her again messed with his head and brought up thoughts better left buried.

The buzzer to his apartment rang, and he punched the button on the keypad that would release the lock on the main entry downstairs.

Doubly glad he'd sent Katrina on her way, he opened the door and waited for the elevator to arrive on the fifteenth floor.

In less than a minute the doors whirred open, and whereas his date's four-inch heels had clacked purposefully across the space, Chloe stepped onto the cream marble floor with the grace of a dancer, not the slightest sound coming from her pale, high-arched feet.

And yep. There it was. The buzzing in his skull that signaled danger.

He blinked and looked closer, realizing what he'd first thought were some kind of flesh-colored shoes were actually nothing of the kind. Pink tipped nails glittered in the hallway light. Even as he stared, she curled her toes under her feet as if trying to hide them. His head cleared in an instant.

What the hell was going on?

Had she been robbed? Assaulted?

His gaze traveled up her slim calves and over her knees and lingered on the hem of her raincoat, a white-knuckled fist keeping the edges together.

Concern erased all traces of irritation. "Chloe, are you okay?"

"Y-yes."

He finally met her eyes and found them bright. Too bright— the blue depths teeming with some terrible emotion.

One glance at the twin mascara tracks running down her delicate face, the swollen bottom lip, and he knew.

Chloe was in trouble. Big trouble.

CHAPTER TWO

CHLOE PERCHED ON the edge of an overstuffed leather couch and took another sip of her whiskey—her second glass—wincing as it hit the sore spot on her lip.

Sitting on the matching ottoman across from her, Brad's eyes glittered with the same dangerous undertones they'd held fifteen minutes ago in the hallway when he'd gently touched the corner of her mouth and asked, "Where is the bastard?"

It had taken her a moment to realize he thought Travis had hit her.

He had. Just not with his fists.

There was no way she could explain the bitter humiliation that clogged her throat, that made her want to crawl away and hide from the world. Not to a man like Brad, who'd gone through girlfriends in droves back in high school. Girls who had been drawn to the same rough-edged smile she'd once been, only hers had been a childish infatuation that had eventually faded away, like a temporary tattoo.

Until the night of her wedding. When a single touch had brought it all roaring back. She'd been mortified at her reaction. Terrified that he'd see the truth in her eyes. Travis had rescued her just in time.

Rescued. That was one way to put it. Especially since her Prince Charming had turned out to be the villain of the story.

She continued to sip her drink, welcoming the fiery warmth that bloomed in her stomach.

"Let me take your coat, at least." Brad's low voice broke through her inner turmoil.

"No!" Her hand went to the tie, fiddling with it. "I—I'm still cold."

What was she going to do? If she stayed the night, he was going to figure out she didn't have much on under the coat. She could crash on Brad's couch, huddled under a blanket— but the image of herself in the hotel bedroom doing much the same thing caused something between a laugh and a cry to exit her throat.

"Okay." He sat straight up, elbows coming off his knees. "Ready to tell me what happened?"

Her glance flickered to Brad's onyx-tiled fireplace. "I already explained. My hotel was overbooked. There were…people staying in the room."

And she could only imagine what those "people" were now doing.

Unless Travis had already passed out, as he tended to do on the nights he'd had too much to drink. Her wedding night had been a disaster. As had the nights that had followed. When her girlfriends had giggled about how many times in a row they'd done you-know-what on their honeymoons, she'd laughed right along with them, all the while wondering if there really was something wrong with her.

Travis's frustration had grown as her response to him had become more and more mechanical—as she'd forced herself to participate. As a result, he'd started working longer hours. To save for their future, he'd said. She'd had no idea her parents had been one of his biggest clients until she'd found some paperwork on his desk—along with some hefty fees they'd paid Travis for managing their investment accounts.

Despite the warning signs, she'd never suspected anything

was off until she came home sick from her night shift at the hospital to hear terrible shrieking noises coming from the bedroom. She'd raced back to find him naked—flat on his back—another woman straddling his hips. He'd pleaded for forgiveness, promised it was a mistake, said it would never happen again.

Stay? Or leave?

She'd decided to fight for her marriage. For eight long months. Tonight had been the *pièce de résistance* in her campaign to rekindle the spark he'd once felt toward her. She'd seduce him.

Only Travis hadn't needed seducing.

He just needed someone other than her.

Her eyes closed, and she took a longer pull on her drink. So much for her two weeks' worth of vacation.

"Hey." The murmured word dragged her back to the surface, even though she just wanted to keep sinking into the mire, never to resurface. "Do you want me to call Jason?"

Her lids parted, and she struggled to focus on the handsome face across from her. "Please don't. He'll just worry."

"He should worry." He nodded toward her feet. "Where are your shoes, Chloe?"

She gnawed the inside of her cheek. Why hadn't she come up with a plausible explanation for that?

Because there wasn't one. Other than the truth, which she wasn't ready to voice.

Why had she ever thought she could "vamp" anyone? Especially her husband, whose rough-and-tumble approach to lovemaking did nothing but leave her feeling sore and inadequate. She was pretty sure the woman in her bed hadn't been crying out in pain, so the problem wasn't with her husband, evidently.

Frigid. The word echoed in her head, the mean nastiness of it making the hair rise on the nape of her neck.

She lifted the glass and found it empty. Held it out.

"I don't think…" Brad began.

Only to stop when she whispered, "Please."

Getting up, he went over to the bar, retrieved a cut-glass decanter of amber liquid and poured some in her glass, the *lug-lug* from the bottle strangely satisfying.

She noticed he didn't refill his own tumbler, just took up his post again and watched her. Her shoulder hitched in an awkward shrug. "If you were in the middle of doing something, don't let me stop you."

She giggled as she said the last word, and her eyes widened. "Sorry. It's been a while." And she'd never been much of a drinker. It was amazing how it dulled the pain, though.

Something she could get used to.

He ignored her comment and said, "Shoes?"

Oh, that's right. He wanted to know what she'd done with her stupid shoes.

"I left them behind, along with all my other little shackles." That rock in her ring hadn't been so little. But then again, her daddy's investment money had probably paid for it, too. Something about that thought made her laugh again.

Brad's hand covered hers, his fingers as warm as fire. Just like the alcohol sloshing around inside her. But when she tried to lift the glass to her lips, it wouldn't move. Because Brad was physically holding her arm in place.

"Hey." She tried to tug free of his grip.

"I think you've had enough for tonight."

"Oh, no. Not nearly enough." Her head felt like some kind of weird flower that when deprived of drink began to wilt… wilt…wilt…until someone watered it again. She snapped it back upright when her forehead touched Brad's muscular arm and tried to burrow into it, a strange lethargy taking hold of her.

Gentle fingers prised hers loose from the glass and set the drink on the wooden floor beside the ottoman. Just as she started to wilt again she felt arms at her back, beneath her knees, and she levitated just like she'd seen in those horror movies when a demon possessed someone's body. But when she tried to hold her arms out to float higher, she found them trapped against her sides.

And while this demon growled in a low, deep voice just like the ones in the films, the tone didn't sound angry. Instead, the soft words circled the air above her face. She pulled them into her lungs, knowing somehow this being was powerful enough to keep all the other demons at bay. Including Travis. Her breath exited again on a sigh, along with the will to do anything but snuggle close and slip away into oblivion.

Brad pushed open the door to his bedroom, thankful he and Katrina had not spent time on the king-sized mattress like he'd planned. Instead, he set Chloe on top of the brown silk coverlet, not quite sure what to do with her. The guest bedroom hadn't been used in ages and he didn't think the bed even had a sheet on under the tan striped spread.

He gazed down at her, something inside him softening as memories from their childhood washed over him. The three of them bobbing in the pool in Jason's parents' backyard, tossing a young Chloe high into the air and hearing her happy scream as she hit the water and sank—then spluttered back to the surface ready for more.

How embarrassed he'd been when his friend's folks had to come to the police station to pick him up when, at eighteen years of age and fed up with life, he'd careened around a dangerous curve on his motorcycle, intent on putting an end to his pain, only to have the damn bike slide out from under him on the unpaved road before he'd hit full speed. When he'd opened his eyes—still very much alive—all he'd been able to think of was that his parents had been right about him: he screwed up everything.

Chloe's parents had dragged him home with them that night.

He could still see the wide-eyed stare Chloe had given him when he'd walked through the front door, road rash burning up one of his cheeks and the side of his right arm. The way she'd covered her mouth with both hands in horror.

That look had convinced him that checking out really would hurt someone—even if his parents had sniffed in disgust and simply sent his chopper off to the nearest repair shop without a word. They'd tended to show their displeasure in an entirely different way—a locked door was a powerful weapon.

Yes, he and Chloe Jenkins had been through a lot together.

But never in his wildest dreams had he pictured her in his bed. Well, maybe he had. But he'd damned himself from here to eternity for wanting to peel off her wedding dress and have her innocence all to himself.

Shaking off the thought, he started to pull one corner of the bedspread around her, but her coat was still wet. He really didn't want her to sleep in it—especially as she'd begun shaking the second she'd entered the apartment, despite the fact that late spring in New York tended toward warm and humid. Her continued shivering was the only reason he'd handed her the glass of whiskey in the first place.

He couldn't do anything about her damp hair—the loose strands a charming melding of blond and red—but he could slip her coat off and at least let her sleep in dry clothes.

His fingers went to the knot at her waist, and he frowned at how tightly she'd cinched the thing. If he'd had any doubts about leaving her in it, that quashed them. He worked at the tie until one loop loosened then slid free. Taking a deep breath, he parted the edges of the coat. The air whistled right back out of his lungs at the sight that met his tired eyes.

Holy hell.

A black negligee—opaque lace on top with a floaty skirt made of some kind of see-through fabric—was all she had on…

well, other than the tiniest pair of panties known to mankind. Panties that were clearly visible. Clearly sheer.

He swallowed hard, torn between the desire to devour her with his eyes and wrap the coat tightly back around her. His body was having a tough time knowing which of his mixed signals to obey, although he might as well finish what he'd started and take the coat the rest of the way off, so she could at least sleep in comfort.

Unlike him, who'd probably have this image seared onto the backs of his eyelids for the rest of his life.

He slid the coat off her, turning her body to the side as he pulled it out from under her. What in God's name had Chloe been thinking, walking around downtown New York like this?

She was the cautious one. The one who'd balked at riding on the back of his motorcycle, even after he'd tamed some of his wilder urges.

And yet here she was. In his apartment, like a sexy flasher from one of those secretary fantasies. She sure as hell hadn't come here to seduce *him* with the get-up.

Then who?

He remembered the smeared mascara. The haunted look in her eyes.

It suddenly became clear in a rush. Jason's random comments about his brother-in-law took on new meaning. How he'd said Chloe never complained but Jason was convinced something was wrong with their marriage and had been for a long time. Travis always seemed to be off somewhere or other on business, leaving Chloe at home alone.

Brad pulled the covers over her, hiding her from his own prying eyes—something that he was now thoroughly ashamed of.

He could almost bet Travis was in a hotel room somewhere in New York. And that Chloe's shoes were there as well. He could easily guess why she'd come to town and what she must have found once she'd arrived. His fingers tightened around the coat in his hands until his knuckles ached as he stared down at her long lashes, the dark circles under her eyes...the slight swelling on her lip.

Damn that man. He'd hurt Chloe.

If it was the last thing Brad did, he was going to make Travis Maroni pay for his sins.

CHAPTER THREE

"I GOT A CALL this morning. He's looking for her."

Jason's worried voice met him as soon as Brad answered his cellphone. He looked up from the case notes of Angel's newest prenatal patient, a thirty-five-year-old woman whose ultrasound scan had revealed a fetal heart defect. The baby was fine *in utero*, but would die within minutes once out of that safe environment if something wasn't done.

To top it all off, he'd arrived at his office that morning to find a snarky resignation letter from Katrina, his date from the previous evening. She'd evidently not been as blasé about being shooed from his apartment as she'd seemed to be at the time.

Which meant his unit was now short-staffed.

That's what he got for getting involved with a colleague. Never again.

"Brad, you still there?"

"Yeah, yeah. Sorry. Just trying to think." That was another thing. There was no way he was going to let Chloe head home before he knew exactly what was going on between her and that scumbag husband of hers. "She wasn't in good shape last night, Jason, which is why I called. I figured you'd be worried."

"I'm glad you did. We had no idea she was even headed to New York. Dad is fit to be tied. Travis swears it's all a big misunderstanding, that Chloe took off after an argument, but he's not fooling anyone. If he weren't my sister's husband…"

Brad's thoughts exactly. "Is he still in New York?"

"No, he's home. Said he was surprised not to find Chloe here. Claims to be worried as hell."

There was no way Brad would have ever left New York without searching every inch of it first. For the man just to drive home without even trying to locate her was unthinkable. What if she'd been mugged…or worse?

"Did you tell him she was at my place?"

"I'm not telling him anything." There was a pause over the line. "Is she okay? Physically, I mean?"

"She seemed to be. She was still asleep when I left this morning." Should he tell Jason about the split lip or what she'd been wearing when she'd shown up at the apartment? He'd laid a pair of exercise sweats and a black T-shirt across the end of his bed. He figured she could pull the laces around the waist tight enough to keep the pants from sliding below the swell of her hips. Which brought his mind right back to those soft curves that were everything a man could want.

Except she was Chloe.

And it was best to keep her racy attire between the two of them—no need for Jason to know. He didn't want to embarrass her any more than necessary.

An idea formed. "Is she still working at the community hospital there in Hartford?" Chloe had graduated from nursing school about the same time he had graduated from med school. She'd even specialized in pediatrics, if he remembered right.

"Yes, why?"

"Can you call them and explain the situation? Ask them to give her some time off?"

"I think she's got some vacation time coming, but I'll check to make sure. Dad invested quite a bit of money in one of their service projects a year or two ago." A chuckle came over the phone. "Chloe just about blew a gasket when she heard, asked him if he was trying to buy a permanent position for her."

Brad could imagine that quite well. He'd been on the receiving end of that outrage a time or two—like when he'd caught her holding hands with a boy on the swing at her parents' house. The glare he'd given the kid had sent him scrambling for the sidewalk. But when he'd tried to give Chloe a stern warning, she'd sniffed and claimed there was nothing to worry about. She'd decided to wait until she got married to "do it."

Did people even do that nowadays?

Evidently they did, because when he'd laughed in her face, she'd flushed scarlet and then balled her fingers into a tight fist before punching him in the chest. Right on top of the fading bruise from his motorcycle accident. It had stung, but it had also gotten her point across: her virginity was no joking matter.

Something his mind had also toyed with the night of her wedding. Had she really saved herself? Only to wind up with a jerk like Travis?

His hand went to the spot and rubbed it as if he could still feel where she'd walloped him. And, really, he could. A circular Celtic symbol—the tree of life at its center—was inked on the very spot his road rash had once covered, starting at his chest and wrapping around the top of his left shoulder. A reminder to always choose life.

Thankfully his polo shirts now covered up that little bit of history. Some of his patients might not understand what the tattoo had come to symbolize.

He shook himself back to the present and Jason's phone call. "I've just had a nurse quit on me. I don't know if Chloe will go for it, but maybe she'd be interested in filling the spot for a while. At least until she can sort through whatever happened with Travis. Or until I can talk the nurse into coming back."

Why was the thought of calling Katrina suddenly distasteful?

"That's a great idea. Maybe she's finally ready to unload the bastard."

"Maybe." Brad scrubbed a hand across his jaw, his eyes going back to the notes on his desk. "I'll let you know what she says. She can stay at the apartment until she decides what she wants to do. It's not easy to get a short-term lease nowadays."

And just why had he offered that? He wasn't exactly celibate, neither did he have any plans to become so. He gave an internal shrug. She was an adult. Surely they could work out some kind of arrangement. After all, it wasn't a permanent thing. Probably a week or two at the most. She might not even go for it—he was beginning to hope she wouldn't, in fact.

But deep down inside something whispered that he was telling the biggest lie of his life. Because he did want her to stay. Wanted to somehow keep her safe from whoever had hurt her.

And if she turned him down and walked away?

He might just have to coax her to change her mind.

"You want me to what?"

Chloe stared across the table at Brad. He was offering her a job? She toyed with the tie on the sweats he'd loaned her and tried to keep her face from flaming in renewed embarrassment. When she'd awoken coatless on a huge king-sized bed with no memory of how she'd gotten there, she'd thought for a panicked second she might have slept with him. His warm masculine scent permeated the space, from the pillow where she'd laid her head to the clothes currently enveloping her body.

But there'd been no sign that he'd slept in the bed, neither was there that familiar morning-after ache—an unpleasant side effect of sex with her husband.

But still. His offer had come out of nowhere.

Brad glanced up from the plate of takeout Yakisoba, brows raised. "One of the nurses in the prenatal unit quit unexpectedly. I wondered if you might want to fill in until we can find a permanent replacement."

"Why?"

"Why not?" He studied her from across the table. "Unless you're anxious to get home."

Dammit. The fire licked along her cheeks again. She had no intention of going home—not that the monstrosity she and Travis had lived in had ever really been home. She'd already contacted a lawyer in Connecticut and started the ball rolling on her divorce. No, you weren't supposed to make any major changes during a crisis, but she'd already decided to leave if her swan dive into the deep end of the seduction pool didn't work.

Swan dive. Right.

Instead of a smooth, clean entry into the water, she'd landed with a belly flop that had been deafening, knocking the wind from her lungs and leaving her clawing her way to the surface.

Well, she was there now, taking her first breath of freedom after six long, suffocating years. She was never submerging herself like that ever again.

Not for anyone.

"I was actually thinking of relocating," she said slowly, the idea taking root and sprouting its first leaf. She could do this.

Unless her father was behind Brad's offer, just like she suspected him of being behind her promotion at the hospital. "Wait, did Daddy call and ask you to hire me?"

Brad's eyes narrowed for a second or two. "Do you think I'm lying to you, Chloe?"

It wouldn't be the first time she'd been lied to. "No, but…"

"But what?"

She licked her lips. "I don't want you doing this because you feel sorry for me." As much as she wanted to, she couldn't seem to hold his gaze, fiddling with her chopsticks instead. "I'm filing for divorce."

"I'm glad."

The low voice caused her head to come up. Some knowing glimmer in the depths of Brad's eyes caused her to bristle. As if he'd expected this outcome all along. "You and Jason never gave him a chance."

"No. But you did."

Yes, and now her brother and Brad were free to gloat about her stupidity behind her back. Wouldn't she, if she were in their place?

Instead, his hand covered hers, the warmth seeping through her icy skin. "Whatever else you might think, I wanted it to work out. Wanted you to be happy."

Just as Jason had. He'd kissed her cheek at the rehearsal dinner and whispered that very thing. "Be happy, little sis."

She swallowed the wave of emotion. Brad had always been there for her, even though he'd never been loud and showy about it. He had always been one of the first people on the scene when something had happened—whether it had been when her sickly appendix had needed to come out, or standing beside her as she'd cried over the grave of Treehouse, her dog.

And later he and Jason had accompanied her on her first official post PADI certification dive off the New Jersey coast, and they'd later explored several local shipwreck sites. She blinked away memories of those muscular legs propelling him through the water with ease, of his fingers gripping hers as he'd tugged her away from areas he'd felt were too dangerous. He'd had no idea that he'd been the most dangerous thing in the ocean. At least to her equilibrium.

Despite those awkward moments, she'd always been able to count on him. Maybe it was time she returned the favor. If he really was in a bind, shouldn't she be willing to lend a hand?

"Thank you." She sighed. "About the position. I would imagine there'd be plenty of nurses ready to jump at the chance to work at Angel's." She loved the hospital's nickname, loved how it seemed to fit, as if the hospital served as the guardian angel of sick children everywhere.

Brad sat back in his chair. "There are, but it'll take time to put out a call for applications and then wade through them all."

"What about an apartment? There's no way I can commute from Hartford." Neither would she want to.

"I thought you might consider staying here. I have an extra bedroom. I'm sure we could stay out of each other's hair."

She bit her lip. Speaking of bedrooms, she'd noticed there was no way to lock the door of his room. Oh, there was a keyhole, but no key to secure it that she could see. The same held true for the bathroom. When she'd looked at the other doors—with the exception of the front door—she'd found the same thing. No keys for any of them. He lived alone, so he probably didn't think anything of it, but if she stayed here she wanted to be able to at least lock the bathroom.

His voice broke through. "What are you thinking?"

She scrambled around for an answer and finally just blurted it out. "Where are your keys?"

"Keys?"

"For all your doors."

His face went utterly still for a second or two then he shrugged. "There's no one else living here, so I haven't felt the need to mess with them."

Just as she'd thought. "But you do have them somewhere, right?"

"I do." There was something strange about the way he answered her, but she couldn't put her finger on it so she tried a different tack.

"Well, what about your life? I don't want to disrupt whatever you've got going on by staying here." She stopped again when his frown deepened. "Are you...um, seeing someone?"

The lines between his brows eased, and one corner of his mouth quirked up. "Not at the moment."

"Oh."

"Even if that situation changes, the apartment has thick walls."

Heat swept up her neck and threatened to shoot from her ears. In other words, she wouldn't hear anything that went on. Maybe not, but her imagination would fill in the blanks. "Are you sure you want me staying—"

"I wouldn't have offered if I didn't mean it." His brows went up. "Unless you don't think you can handle it."

The battle cry from their younger years hung in the air between them. The only time she hadn't risen to one of those challenges had been when he'd rolled up next to her on his motorcycle, fresh from getting his medical license, and had dared her to take a victory lap around town with him. The thought of being pressed tight against his back, her inner thighs gripping his, had made something dangerous shimmy through her abdomen—the exact sensation she'd experienced when they'd danced at her wedding. It had brought a wariness that was even stronger than her fear of motorcycles.

She'd gulped before chickening out—blaming it on his long-forgotten accident in high school.

And now? Was she still chicken?

With those light green eyes watching her every move, trying to ferret out any exposed weakness? She'd vowed to give herself a brand-new start. To do that—and to survive her time with Brad—she needed to live by a whole new set of rules. His. And if he could throw down the gauntlet, she would just pick it up and twirl it over her head.

Dropping her chopsticks onto her plate, she leaned forward, all too aware that she was dressed in the man's clothes and was about to agree to live in his home. But that was small potatoes. She'd survived the horror of knowing he'd seen her body in all its questionable glory last night—and he'd evidently been unmoved by the sight. So they were good to go.

"As long as I can have a key to my bedroom and the bathroom, I think I can handle it all right," she said sweetly. "But... can you?"

CHAPTER FOUR

THE JEANS FIT PERFECTLY.

Of course they would. Brad could probably tell a woman's clothing size with a single glance. And the smoky-green belted top did make the blue of her eyes stand out. She couldn't remember the last time Travis had bought her an article of clothing.

Not that she'd wanted him to. She assumed men didn't like doing that sort of thing, unless it was buying slinky lingerie.

Well, in reality, Brad had had no choice. It wasn't like she could go shopping in the get-up she'd arrived in—which she'd stuffed in a plastic bag and thrown right in the trash. The fewer reminders she had of that night the better. Even so, answering the door and finding Brad's doorman standing there with a wrapped package in his hand had been a surprise. Swallowing her pride and accepting his offer hadn't been easy.

But at least it meant she could go out and shop for her own clothing...including hospital gear. Brad said scrubs were the order of the day, the funkier the better. And true to his word he'd produced two shiny new keys, one for her bedroom and one for the bathroom, so she could at least dress and bathe in private.

A spark of excitement zipped through her. Brand-new scrubs were fitting for a brand-new life. This was the perfect opportunity to start over. The lawyer she'd spoken with had assured her she'd only need to face Travis one more time...across the courtroom when the divorce was finalized.

Although there was a certain amount of guilt swirling around inside of her over her failed marriage, she felt more relief than anything. No more worrying about showing enough enthusiasm in bed or fearing the slightest twitch of discomfort would bring about one of Travis's long-suffering sighs.

She checked out the view from behind in the full-length mirror in Brad's bedroom, carefully avoiding glancing at the expanse of reflective glass mounted on the ceiling over that huge bed. Somehow she didn't think he used it for shaving.

Chloe shuddered. At least her ex had never suggested putting mirrors in their bedroom. Her eyes tracked to the bed again, the image of Brad's muscular frame sweeping through her mind, the tattoo across his shoulder bunching with each movement.

Her mouth went dry. She closed her eyes and tried to remember exactly what that tattoo looked like. It had been some kind of jagged circle enclosing a tree. As a teenager, her eyes had gone to it again and again as he'd sprawled out on a lounge chair by her parents' pool. Even then he'd cut a powerful figure. No wonder she'd had a crush on him.

But as gorgeous as he was, there'd been a raw, untamed quality to him that had frightened her at times. Travis had been smooth and refined...steady and safe in comparison, which had been what she'd thought she wanted.

She gave a pained laugh. Boy, were appearances deceptive. Travis had been anything but safe.

At least now she was free.

Digging in her handbag, she located her phone and sent Brad a text thanking him for the clothes and letting him know she was headed out to go shopping for some new things. He'd promised to take her to the hospital tomorrow to show her the prenatal wing and introduce her to the staff.

Just as she got ready to head to the lobby and ask the doorman to hail a cab, the phone rang. She stared at it, wondering if she should answer it or let the machine pick up. But maybe Brad had gotten her text and was calling her to firm up times for dinner or something.

She lifted the receiver from its cradle. "Hello?"

There was a pause then a woman's voice came through. "Who is this?"

Uh-oh. That was *not* a happy tone.

"Chloe Jenkins. I'm a...friend of Brad's." It was true, right? "He's not here right now, though. Can I take a message?"

"This is Katrina. I wanted to see if he got the note I left him."

Note? Brad hadn't mentioned anything about one. But why would he? Those mirrors came back to her thoughts. Of course. This was probably one of Brad's "women."

"I...um. I'm not sure." How was this for awkward? "I can leave him a message and let him know you called."

"Don't bother." If anything, the woman's voice had grown even colder. "He's got my number. If he wants me, he can call me."

Chloe gulped. If he wanted her? Did she mean as in beneath the mirrors?

Oh, lordy. This could get really weird if a parade of women started trekking through at all hours of the night.

The sound of the dial tone in her ear told her the lady in question hadn't even bothered to say goodbye before hanging up. But, then, why would she? This Katrina person didn't even know who she was.

She dropped the phone back onto its stand, making a mental note not to pick it up again. Ever. Otherwise someone could get the wrong idea about why *she* was staying here. She had no intention of becoming part of Brad's female entourage.

Actually, the woman's call had come at the perfect time

because she needed to remind herself of her reasons for being there. It was to get away from Travis, not to dive head first back into the dating pool.

Although from Travis's cutting remarks about her prowess in the bedroom she might not need to worry about that for a long time to come. She certainly didn't want to relive any of those awful moments, especially with a stranger.

She'd have to eventually, though. She didn't want to go through life alone. She wanted children. A family. It's why she'd gotten married in the first place, to have what her parents had. A love that endured for decades.

Maybe she could talk to someone about her difficulties in that area. She certainly couldn't talk to Jason, not only because he'd always despised Travis but because of the ick factor involved. And the few girlfriends she had couldn't really give her a man's point of view—other than claiming Travis was a jerk who was terrible in bed. But was he? Other women seemed to like his moves just fine, judging from the bimbo who'd been hanging all over him at the hotel. So the problem had to be with her.

But how to fix it…

She glanced at the phone, remembering Katrina's irked voice. Brad had been with lots of women. And Katrina's attitude indicated that they didn't mind the instant replays. They *wanted* to be with him. Were peeved when they couldn't be.

What better person to pinpoint where she'd gone wrong with Travis and give her some pointers on how to act in any future relationships. It wouldn't be strange, right? The two of them had been friends since childhood. He had no idea she'd had a crush on him during their teenage years. And his experience with the female sex could give her insights that a stranger might be too embarrassed to be honest about. Brad could always be counted on to tell it like it was. No sugar coating involved with that man.

She took a deep breath and let it out. That settled it, then. She'd broach the subject somehow and see how he reacted. If he acted like it was no big deal, she'd pick his brain and try to figure out exactly what a man wanted from a woman.

Because, whatever it was, she didn't have it…and she had no idea where to get it.

Brad stood in the observation room above the surgical suite and watched as the surgeon prepped his patient for a hysterotomy. It was the same procedure his fetal heart patient would have to undergo in a month or two, except this particular fetal surgery was being done to close a neural tube defect and avoid a woman giving birth to a child with physical deficits. Few open fetal surgeries were done each year because of the risks to the baby, but Angel's was considered one of the best facilities in the country. People came to them from all over the U.S.

He shifted to the right to get a better view as the skilled fingers of the surgeon reached the uterus and prepared to open it.

Cade Coleman, the newest member of Angel's surgical staff, had been called in to perform the delicate procedure, and while Brad could acknowledge the man's expertise, he and the surgeon had already butted heads during the few weeks he'd been at the hospital.

Including the timing of the current surgery.

Brad didn't know exactly how Coleman had been appointed second in command without even a trial period, but the man evidently had some pull with Angel's resident neurosurgeon, Alex Rodriguez, although Brad couldn't imagine anyone forcing Alex's hand on anything. There'd been rumors of a secret meeting between the two, which Brad had initially shrugged off as gossip. But something had gone down because Alex hadn't quite been able to meet Brad's eyes when he'd told him the news.

Hell, could life get any more complicated? First Chloe

showed up on his doorstep, her wounded eyes revealing far more than she knew. Then Katrina wigged out on him just as the prenatal wing was heading into its busiest season. Throw a hard-headed surgeon into the mix and Brad had his hands full.

Perfect.

Using the controls to zoom in on the surgical site, he watched the monitor as Cade reached into Melanie Roberts's womb with gloved fingers and gently drew the fetus into view. A boy. Melanie probably already knew that, though, through the wonders of ultrasound. The same test that had revealed the defect.

Turning the baby to expose the bubble-like formation on his lower spine, Coleman's magnifying goggles zeroed in on the problem—the tiny camera mounted on his headgear giving Brad the same clear view. The defect was about an inch long, close to the base of the spine, but despite the location, the open portion of the back could still cause problems with the child's lower limbs if not corrected. At twenty-one weeks, the fetus's kick reflex was still strong and healthy, the perfect time to operate, according to Coleman.

As if feeling Brad's eyes on him, Cade glanced toward the huge bank of windows to his right. The magnified view of the operating room on a second monitor only made the furrows visible above the surgeon's goggles seem that much deeper. No doubt it rankled to have to answer to someone else when he'd run his own department in LA. But if you moved hospitals, you couldn't expect to start at the top. And if the man had any illusions about replacing Brad, he had another think coming. If either of them left, it would be Coleman.

Brad looked up from the monitor and gave the other man a slight nod to indicate he'd seen the problem and agreed with whatever Cade saw fit to do. The surgeon turned back to his tiny patient and Brad's thoughts went back to Chloe.

Hell, he'd talked to Jason again that morning and almost the first thing out of his friend's mouth had been a stern reminder that Chloe was still his little sister. As if Brad didn't know that.

What did Jason expect him to do? Make a move on her? Impossible.

Unbidden, his brain played back the sight he'd uncovered when he'd taken off Chloe's coat. His reaction had been anything but brotherly. Neither had his reaction to seeing her stroll through the apartment in his sweat pants the next morning. But he was practically a family member—kind of like a first cousin, right?—and he'd better remember it. Chloe was fragile right now. Vulnerable. He, more than anyone, should remember what it was like to be rejected by those who were supposed to love you unconditionally—but who, instead, were completely indifferent to your efforts to please them.

Just like Travis had been with Chloe's efforts? Something inside him said yes, that's exactly what had happened. She'd gone there dressed in an outfit that should have had the man salivating like a hungry hyena. It had certainly gotten a reaction out of *him*. Instead, Travis had done or said something that had cut her to the quick.

Something that had caused her to flee into the night.

Brad didn't want to be that man. Didn't want to hurt someone who'd once meant a lot to him.

Someone who still did. Sweet innocent, idealistic Chloe.

One wrong move on his part and he could hurt her even more. Especially if he couldn't keep himself in check. If anything could keep him on the straight and narrow, that realization should.

At least, he hoped it would.

CHAPTER FIVE

HE HAD TO BE KIDDING.

Resting on Brad's bent thigh was a dark shiny helmet that matched the one currently on his head, the visor flipped up so he could see her. And he was seated—booted foot casually propped up on the left pedal—on top of a motorcycle. One that looked eerily familiar. When he'd said he'd meet her in the parking garage this morning, she'd assumed he'd be pulling up next to her in a Beamer, not on a Harley.

He could have stepped right out of one of her old photos from days gone by. She'd thought that with all his success his old mode of transportation would have been one of the first things to go. Evidently some things never changed. Was that really his old motorcycle? The one he'd had his accident on? A shiver of fear went through her.

"I—I can't ride on that."

His mouth quirked, and he held out the helmet. "I'll be careful. Promise." The black leather jacket he wore—along with a second one draped on the seat behind him—said otherwise. The pair screamed danger with a capital D.

Gripping the strap of her purse as if it alone could save her, she said, "Don't you have a car, like normal doctors?"

"Since when have I ever done things that others deem 'normal'?"

Was he referring to his parents? They'd always disapproved

of Brad's motorcycle riding, although she'd never heard them say anything outright. But she'd overheard Jason talking to their mom and dad once about how Brad felt more at home at their house than at his own. Jason had said he could see why. Brad's folks were a matched set—snooty, looking down their noses at anything that didn't meet with their approval. Their own son was high on that list, evidently, since they looked right through him, instead of at him.

Chloe hesitated. Yes, Brad knew she was afraid of motorcycles, especially after she'd seen the damage done by his accident. But did she really want him to put her in the same category as his parents...thinking she was too good to be seen riding on one?

His gaze slid across her cheeks. Touched lower. "I'll take good care of you, Chloe. I give you my word." He balanced the helmet on his leg again then reached out his hand, palm up.

She licked her lips, then, as if hypnotized, she put her fingers in his and let him tug her a few steps closer until his knee touched the side of her thigh. Another shiver went through her, this one having nothing to do with fear but something even worse.

Could she really ride on that thing, behind him? She'd balked once before. Not just because of her fear but because of how unpredictable her reactions to him were. And the feeling that she'd be betraying Travis if she let her guard down, even for a second.

Knowing what she did now, that naïve sentiment was laughable.

Travis was no longer a part of her life, and he never would be again. So shouldn't she get out and see exactly what she'd been missing?

But...on a motorcycle?

Why the hell not?

Lifting her chin, she grabbed the helmet from his leg, turned

it round and jammed it on her head. The sense of claustrophobia was immediate, as was the urge to claw the thing back
off again.

*It's supposed to cradle your head, dummy, how else is it
going to protect you?*

Maybe he noticed her panic because Brad put down the
kickstand and hauled the bike back onto it, before swinging his
leg over the seat and standing in front of her. Placing his hands
on her shoulders and turning her to face him, he took hold of
the straps on either side of the helmet and fastened them, ad-
justing the fit, his warm fingers grazing her throat repeatedly.
He pushed her visor up and tilted her head so he could peer in
at her. "How does it feel?"

Oh, baby. Did he mean the helmet or his touch?

Don't be ridiculous. Of course he's talking about the helmet.

"Tight. Hot."

His Adam's apple dipped, and he stared at her for a moment,
before answering. "It's supposed to be snug."

His voice was a little rougher than it had been a moment
ago. Had she said something stupid? Or maybe he was having second thoughts about riding with her. "Are you sure this
is a good idea?"

He gave a low laugh. "I thought so up until a few seconds
ago."

"How long will it take to reach the hospital?"

"Depending on traffic, about fifteen minutes."

"Okay. Let's get this over with."

He nodded, handing her the second jacket and waiting until
she'd zipped it up. His warm scent clung to the leather, and it
was all she could do not to close her eyes and breathe it deep
into her lungs. The fact that it was there, surrounding her,
gave her a dose of courage that had been sorely missing a few
seconds ago. He'd promised to take care of her, and Brad had
never gone back on a promise that she knew of.

Getting back on the motorcycle, Brad pushed it forward and eased up the kickstand. "There are footrests just behind mine. So climb up and hang on."

Tightening her resolve, she walked the couple of steps it took to reach him then steadied herself by putting a hand on his shoulder. Pretending she was mounting a horse, she swung her leg over the back of the seat, trying to sit as far back as possible—which proved *im*possible. The thing was angled so that she slid forward until her tummy was pancaked against his back.

This was going to be the longest fifteen minutes of her life.

"Can you hear me?" The low voice in her ear made her jerk, until she realized it was coming through her helmet. Brad must have some kind of built-in walkie-talkie system that let him communicate with whoever was on the back.

He'd ridden double like this before. Often enough to buy special helmets. Why did the thought make a warning hiss go off in her head?

"Chloe?"

She forced her lips to move. "I can hear you."

"There should be a mike below the strap. Swing it up to the front."

Finding a hard plastic object coming off the side of the helmet, she adjusted it so that it was in front of her mouth. "Better?"

"Yep." He rolled the motorcycle forward a few feet and Chloe scrambled to put her hands on his waist. "When we start moving, you're going to want to hang on tighter than that, okay?"

Tighter than she already was? She felt like her fingers were digging into the firm muscles of his sides as it was. "Got it."

Feeling around for the footrests, she planted her feet on them, just as Brad turned a key and the motorcycle rumbled to life beneath her. With the helmet on, it wasn't nearly as loud as she'd expected it to be.

"Okay. When the garage door opens, we'll be on our way. Keep your feet up, even at stops, and lean into the turns."

"Check." She couldn't stop a little giggle. She knew he had to instruct her on how to ride, but she'd never dreamed that three days after her disastrous trip to Travis's hotel room she'd be on her way to a new job and the start of a new life. Even the shuddery fear she felt about riding with Brad couldn't erase her elation. This was the right decision. She felt it in her bones.

The garage door to the apartment building slid up, and Brad revved the engine and rolled through them at a reasonable speed. Nothing like the showy skids and hot-dogging he'd once done to impress the high-school girls. Still, her heart jumped into her throat as he turned left and entered the morning snarl of traffic—the sounds of car engines and buses periodically rupturing the bubble of silence created by her helmet.

On the first real turn she instinctively wrapped her arms around Brad's waist, realizing he was right. She needed to hold on and try to lean when he did. The best way to do that was to be physically connected to him, in much the same way as she'd moved with the horse she'd had years ago. Her hips slid forward even more, pressing intimately against him, her thighs squeezing his in order to maintain her balance. Every inch of her was aware of every inch of him. At first she put it down to basic survival instinct, but that weird tingle down low had nothing to do with survival.

Then Brad turned another corner, wiping away every thought except hanging on, probably much tighter than necessary.

During the first few minutes she was too afraid to move, but once she got used to the vibration from the engine beneath her and the easy way Brad handled the big bike, she began to loosen up a bit and enjoy the ride.

They stopped for a red light. Brad's feet hit the ground to keep them stable, and Chloe drew in a deep breath, noticing the claustrophobia she'd felt earlier was almost gone.

"You okay back there?"

"So far, so good. It's not as bad as I thought it would be." It wasn't quite a lie.

A soft laugh came through. "And I never thought I'd see the day when Chloe Jenkins would agree to ride on my bike."

A reference to her refusal years ago? She smiled, her heart lightening for the first time. "The times are a-changin'."

"Hmm. Want to learn to ride one?"

Her stomach did a back flip. "Yeah, well, the times aren't changing that much. I think I'm going to stick with being a passenger. A bad one."

He reached back to squeeze her leg. "You're doing great."

The light turned green, and Brad revved the engine enough to take off. Her arms instinctively wrapped around him once again, the fingers of her left hand gripping her other one in a vise. It was better than having her palms splayed across his rock-hard abs—a position that seemed far too intimate. Sure, they'd horsed around when they'd been younger and had done plenty of touching. But this was different, although Brad didn't seem affected by it at all.

Despite the concern he'd shown on the night of her arrival, he'd soon reverted to type, viewing the world through a lens of amused cynicism.

Although traffic was bumper to bumper, they were moving at a fairly steady pace and before she knew it they'd cleared Central Park, where green gave way to a pristine white building. Even from her perch Chloe could see the hospital off to their left. "Is there underground parking?"

"There is for our patients. There are a couple of lots near the hospital where we can park, which is what I do on the days I drive to work."

"Isn't that expensive?" Chloe had assumed everyone parked on hospital grounds. But things in New York City were evidently different than they were in Connecticut.

"Staff gets a discount." There was a pause as Brad pulled into a lot across the street from the hospital. "I sometimes take the subway to work, but I didn't think you'd be too anxious to get back on it."

She blinked. "How did you know I rode the subway?"

"My doorman said you had that shell-shocked look of first-time riders."

Little did he know that the shock had been from something very different. Although the fact that Brad had ridden to work just for her touched her. "Thank you. But I'll be okay. Let me at least help with the parking costs."

A suited valet came forward, eyes wide as he looked from them to the bike. He quickly found his professionalism, reaching out a hand to help Chloe off. Her legs were shaking, much to her chagrin, but she smiled at the man anyway. When she glanced at Brad, she noticed his frown, even through the shaded visor. He put down the kickstand and yanked off his helmet, taking the keys from the ignition.

When she fumbled around for the catch to her own helmet, both men moved forward, but the valet stopped almost immediately when Brad handed him the key and held up his hospital ID. "We'll be here until around seven."

The valet nodded, glancing one last time at Chloe before handing Brad a ticket.

Once the man had started the motorcycle and driven into the lot, Brad turned back to her and unsnapped her helmet. She squinched her nose. "I don't even want to think about what my hair looks like. I'm not going to make a very good first impression."

Before she had a chance to do anything about it, warm fingers were brushing damp locks from her forehead and her cheeks and restoring order to her side part. "You could never make a bad impression, Chloe."

That's what he thought. He'd never had her in bed.

Her brows tightened. That was all behind her now. It was time to move on, and she intended to do just that. Maybe she'd even flirt with the first attractive man who came across her path.

Her glance went to Brad and then skipped away. Yikes! Just the thought of flirting with him sent a zing of panic shooting through her chest. Along with a dangerous sense of anticipation that left her breathless. Yep, dangerous was a good word for what she was feeling.

She'd promised herself she'd ask him some pointed questions about men and how their minds worked, but could she really go through with it? Especially after the way she'd felt on the back of his bike?

Maybe she'd test out her theory with the *second* attractive man who came across her path. Just in case. Until she could finally work up the courage to look Brad in the eye and demand he tell her everything he knew.

CHAPTER SIX

"CHLOE, THIS IS Layla Woods, head of our general pediatric department."

The slender blonde standing just inside the hospital lobby held out her hand with a friendly smile. "Nice to meet you. Brad says you're joining his team on the fourth floor."

Chloe wasn't sure how to answer that question. Brad had made it pretty clear he was still looking for someone to take the previous nurse's place. Besides, she'd be going back to her old job at the end of her vacation. "I'm helping out. Temporarily."

She took a moment to glance around. Not only was the lobby big, with glossy marble floors and brightly painted walls, it was also refreshingly cool. Chloe welcomed the chilly air blowing across her heated body. Part of the warmth was due to the city streets, but some of it was also from riding behind her new boss. The crowded subway was sounding better and better.

A red-wigged Raggedy Ann stood a few feet away, cheerfully directing patients and visitors to different wings of the hospital. Well, that was different. But she liked the upbeat, bustling atmosphere of the entryway. Almost a reflection of the city itself.

"Well, it's good to have you," Layla said, bringing her attention back. "I'm new to Angel's too, so if you have any questions, holler. It's probably something I've already asked."

Brad's phone went off, and he glanced down at the readout

with a frown. "I need to get this, sorry. As Layla said, we're up on the fourth floor, if you want to make your way there. They're expecting you."

The other woman tutted at him. "You can't just abandon her. I'll show her around and then take her up myself."

"Thanks. I appreciate it." He punched a button on his phone. "See you in a few."

"Okay."

Standing next to Layla, Chloe suddenly felt big and clunky, even though she was only an inch or two taller than the other woman. But where the pediatrician was made up of subtle curves and well-defined angles, Chloe's hips and boobs were definitely rounder. In shoe terms, Layla was a graceful strappy sandal, while Chloe was a sensible pump.

She sighed. No wonder Travis had gone looking elsewhere.

"You ready?" Another wide smile accompanied the question, and Chloe relaxed. There was nothing snooty or haughty about Layla. Just kindness that shone through her eyes. Along with a strange tinge of sadness.

Everyone had their own problems, she supposed.

The hospital was huge, and Layla's tour took a little longer than expected. When Chloe glanced down at her watch, hoping she wasn't going to get in trouble for being late, the other woman touched her hand. "It's okay. I'm sure Brad's let them know that you're with me."

Chloe nodded and peeked inside the washroom door that Layla had pushed open. "Are you from New York?" she asked.

"Texas. You?"

"Connecticut."

"That's closer to home, at least."

Too close. Chloe gave a pained laugh, horrified to feel the prick of tears. "You know, right now I wish home *was* in Texas."

Layla pulled her into the restroom, peering beneath the stall doors to make sure they were empty. "Are you okay?"

Shaking her head in exasperation at herself, she said, "Not really. But I will be."

One gentle squeeze to the arm later Chloe found words tumbling from her mouth that she had never dreamed of telling anyone. Certainly not her brother or Brad. But something about the other woman—maybe the wise eyes that seemed to see everything—drew the festering poison from her inner wounds like a healing salve. She finished her story with, "I'm filing for divorce."

Layla gave her a quick hug. "It seems we're alike in more ways than one. Remind me to tell you about it some time." She sighed and shook her head. "But for now I think we need to get you upstairs."

When Chloe peeked at her watch again, she was horrified to see an hour had passed since Brad had left her. "I'm so sorry. I'm sure you have other things to do."

"I'm glad I was here when you came in. I haven't…" Her words trailed off. "Well, that's for another day. If you want to, we can get together for drinks some time. O'Malley's is just round the corner. It's a regular haunt for those of us at Angel's."

"Thank you. That sounds great." Maybe starting over wouldn't be as hard as she'd feared. If the job worked out, Brad might consider keeping her on. Surely Layla or someone could point her in the direction of a reasonably priced apartment. Or someone in need of a roommate.

Because Brad wasn't going to want her to live with him for ever. And she shouldn't want that either. Not after all that weirdness she'd felt on the back of his motorcycle.

If that feeling grew…

She rolled her eyes as they made their way to the elevator.

She would just ask him those questions she'd thought about earlier and then get out of his life. And sooner was looking a whole lot better than later.

* * *

It made his blood boil.

Maybe that old expression was true after all, because where there'd been one irritated bubble floating around a moment ago, there was now a steady stream of them rolling up and down the veins of his arms. Filling his chest. Gathering in his skull.

He scowled at the nurses' desk, where Cade Coleman stood talking to none other than Chloe. *His* Chloe.

Okay, she wasn't his. But she was under his care—which was something he never thought he'd say about a woman. And there was something about the way she looked at Cade from beneath her lashes. The ready smile that curved her lips. The color blooming along her cheeks.

His eyes narrowed when she took a strand of hair and twirled it round her index finger.

He'd been on the receiving end of plenty of hair twirls. It usually meant one thing.

Surely she didn't find the guy attractive.

Well, she sure as hell hadn't looked at *him* that way.

As for Coleman, what was he doing, making a move on one of his nurses? One who had only been here for three days.

Whatever it was, he was going to nip it in the bud because Jason would be crawling all over him if he let someone take advantage of Chloe.

"Is there a problem here?"

Chloe's glance went to his, and she jerked upright, the lock of hair falling from her fingers to join the rest of the glossy strands. "I was just…just…" If her cheeks had been pink before, they were flaming now.

What was going on?

Cade, whose elbow had been resting on the counter, casually raised a brow. "No problem. We just hadn't been formally introduced yet."

An oversight Brad hadn't even attempted to rectify. There

was something about the surgeon that made his hackles rise. In all honesty, it was probably because they were both stubborn and opinionated and used to being in charge. Tensions had been high ever since he'd joined the team, but Brad had figured as long as they each stuck to his own job and didn't get in the way of the other, they'd be able to coexist peacefully. Not if Chloe's well-being was at stake, however.

"Chloe?"

She shrugged, her hands clasped on top of the desk. "Like he said, we were just getting to know each other."

Brad's jaw tightened further. Definitely no hair-twirling going on when she spoke to him. But there was a whole lot of guilt in her eyes.

What the hell was she playing at?

Before he could say anything further, Cade rapped his knuckles lightly on the desk, making Chloe jump. "Well, now that we've become a little better acquainted, I'll let you get back to it. I have a few patients to see. I'll talk to you later."

With a brusque nod in Brad's direction he headed for the elevators across from the nurses' station.

"So?" His attention went back to Chloe.

"Can we please talk about this later?"

His brows went up. "If I knew what the hell 'this' was, I'd feel a whole lot better."

"It's nothing. I just don't know how to…" She shook her head and looked away.

Sliding his fingers under her chin, he coaxed her gaze back to his. "You don't know how to what?"

She licked her lips. "Flirt."

The word was so low he wasn't sure he'd heard it correctly. "I'm sorry, did you say flirt?"

The word set his teeth on edge. And sent his thoughts racing.

Tugging from his grip, she wrapped her arms around her

waist, eyes flashing. "I know it must seem stupid to you, but it was one of the reasons…"

One of the other nurses came to the station and settled into a chair, smiling at both of them, obviously unaware of the tense undercurrents.

But at least that angry bubbling sensation inside Brad's chest had eased. Chloe wasn't really interested in Cade. At least, he didn't think she was.

"When does your shift end?"

Ginny, the other nurse, spoke up. "I've been trying to get her to leave for the last half-hour."

"You're already off duty?"

"I feel funny just…leaving."

The pause before "leaving" was telling. She didn't want anyone to know where she was staying. Kind of hard since the address she'd given to Human Resources was his. For the second time in a week he wondered if housing Chloe was a good idea. But he was already committed to this course, and Jason was counting on him.

Tread carefully, bud. If she wanted to keep their living arrangements secret, then he'd better honor that decision.

"I have one other patient to see, and then I'm off as well."

Chloe nodded. "I'll see you later, then."

"Sounds good."

Walking away from the station, he tried to get his head screwed back on straight. But it was tough, because Chloe and Cade weren't his only worries right now. Katrina hadn't quite dropped out of the picture, like he'd hoped she would. She'd not only called and spoken to Chloe, she'd left an angry message on his voice mail. She'd also stopped in at the hospital and had been none too pleased—according to Ginny—to find they'd already replaced her.

It reaffirmed his decision to keep personal and business relationships in two separate compartments. Which made things with Chloe even more complicated. Because the contents of those particular compartments were oozing from minuscule cracks, mingling with each other.

Unlike Katrina, who'd begun on the business end of the spectrum and moved over to the personal, Chloe was the opposite. And if he wasn't careful he'd mess things up not only with her but with her whole family. That was the last thing he wanted to do. He cared about the Jenkins clan. And he and Jason went even further back.

They were the one steady thing in his life. The only relationship he hadn't somehow screwed up.

Yet.

CHAPTER SEVEN

"How are you feeling today?"

Chloe checked Melanie Roberts's IV drip. About six months pregnant, with pink cheeks and a glowing complexion, she seemed the picture of health. Looks could be deceiving, though, because hidden deep within her there'd been a serious problem that had needed to be fixed.

Just like Chloe.

With Melanie's unborn baby afflicted with spina bifida, Cade had been forced to operate on her a few days ago and all had gone well, according to reports. She'd need to stay in the hospital for a few more days to make sure she didn't go into premature labor, and then she'd have to continue on meds to keep her uterus from reacting to the trauma of surgery. Bed rest for the next couple of months. But so far so good. Although they wouldn't know for sure until after she delivered, the baby's prognosis for a normal life was excellent.

Melanie glanced at the IV. "Are you sure the pain medication isn't going to hurt the baby?"

Putting her hand on the woman's shoulder, she gave her a smile. "I'm sure your doctor is being extremely careful. Have you seen him today?"

"Dr. Coleman came in to check on me. And my regular obstetrician is supposed to come by this afternoon."

Chloe busied herself with fluffing pillows and tucking blankets to hide the warmth in her cheeks as Cade's name was mentioned. She'd thought Brad would burst a blood vessel when he'd seen her at the desk yesterday with the surgeon. It had been then that she'd realized that instead of charming Cade with her attempts at flirting she'd been making a fool of herself. Again. When Brad had got her to confess, his brows had drawn together. She'd thought he was going to say something more, but then Ginny had come back to the nurses' station and conversation had fizzled before dying completely.

He'd met her after work, but instead of riding home on his motorcycle he'd put her in a cab and said he'd see her at the apartment. He hadn't. Because as soon as she'd arrived, she'd gone straight to the guest room. Brad hadn't knocked on the door, although she'd known he'd arrived as well. A half-hour later, though, she'd heard the front door open and close. He'd gone out and stayed out until the wee hours of the morning.

Had he been with the nurse who'd called her the other day? It was none of her business if he had. Still, a tiny bloom of hurt had come to life.

She forced her attention back to her patient. "Did you ask Dr. Coleman about your medication?"

"He said it was fine, that the baby shouldn't be affected. It's just that…" she twisted the blankets "…it's just been such a shock. I took the prenatal vitamins just like I was told to. Weren't they supposed to prevent this?"

"Sometimes these things happen, no matter what you do."

Like her impending divorce? If she'd tried harder, done more of what she knew Travis liked in bed, could she have prevented him from getting it elsewhere?

That had been the problem. She had tried. But being coerced to perform had meant she had never been given the chance to try new things of her own free will. To give to him spontaneously from a heart full of love. Instead, his overtures had been more like a boss issuing orders: *No, not there…here. Harder.*

Keep going. There had been no cuddling, no slow build-up of passion. It had been all or nothing with Travis. And even when she'd given it her all, she'd gotten little or nothing in return.

She shook herself out of the memories as she finished up with the patient and went back into the hallway. She was free of that now. Free of treating sex like a duty that she dreaded. Which was why she'd been shocked at the tingling she'd felt sitting behind Brad on the bike. You'd think she'd never respond to another man again. Especially not this soon.

Maybe it was just her hormones urging her to procreate. But she'd never felt the need to have kids with Travis. And he'd never pressed that issue either. Another thing to be glad of.

But she did want children eventually, which meant, unless she wanted to embark on that particular journey alone, she'd have to wade into the dating pool again, the sooner the better.

Only this time she wasn't committing until she was sure she wasn't going to wind right back up where she'd been for the last six years. She wanted someone she shared common ground with. Maybe even someone in the medical field.

Brad's image came to mind, and she pushed it back down. No. He wasn't a better choice than Travis had been. He skipped from woman to woman without a care in the world. Only where Travis had merely broken her pride, if she was honest with herself, Brad could break something much deeper.

No, she needed someone steady and even-tempered. Someone who wasn't cocky or arrogant. Someone who didn't spin out on his motorcycle and nearly kill himself.

Someone... She wrinkled her nose when the word "boring" twirled around in her skull, dancing out of reach every time she tried to grab it and kick it to the curb.

Cade wasn't boring. But he also wasn't someone she could see herself being seriously interested in. It had been fun to try to kid around with him, at least until Brad had made her feel like an idiot.

Why did he even care?

The elevator doors swished open and the man himself exited. Her legs tensed, ready to pivot and hurry away in the other direction. Then their eyes met and it was too late. He made his way over to her.

"How's your day going?"

"Pretty well. I just finished checking on Melanie Roberts. She asked whether the pain meds could affect the baby."

"Did you ask Dr. Coleman about it?"

Strange, the way he always referred to the surgeon by his last name. Almost as if he didn't like the man. "I haven't seen him today. But if I do, I will." She bit her lip. "Would you mind talking to her in the meantime? I think it would put her mind at ease."

"Sure." He glanced at the nurses' desk and then back at her. "Did you stay in last night?"

She decided to play dumb, as if she hadn't noticed he'd stayed out half the night. "I don't know what you mean."

"Did you eat dinner?"

Jerking her eyes away from his, she lifted her chin. "I did. I went out."

She had technically gone round the corner to grab a burger, but she knew her words could be easily misconstrued. Knew she'd phrased them that way on purpose. But something about the way he'd left her alone had stung, and she was desperate for him not to find out how much. He hadn't been home, so there's no way he'd know she'd eaten by herself. Just like she had in the later stages of her marriage.

"Oh?" His fingers scrubbed the side of his jaw. "Have a good time?"

"I did." She decided to do a little probing of her own. "How about you? Do anything interesting?"

"Not really. Took a ride. Saw the city lights."

Sure he had. She noticed he didn't mention whether he'd

taken that ride alone or not. "I'm sure they were pretty." She could only hope the sarcastic edge she'd given her words had been lost on him.

"They were. I'd have invited you to come along, but I know my bike makes you nervous. Didn't think I should push my luck by asking you to do it again."

Was that why he'd sent her home in a cab? He thought she was chicken? She was, but not for the reasons he thought.

"I think you might be surprised."

One of his brows went up. The left one. Why had Chloe never noticed those permanent little lines above it that came from repeating the gesture over the years?

"So you've decided you like motorcycles now?"

Definitely not. But she'd felt safe tucked up against his back. Among other things. But that was something she was never going to admit.

"Let's just say it was tolerable."

"Just what every man wants to hear."

The smile that had started to form on her lips slunk away. No, it probably wasn't what men wanted to hear. Even if it was true.

She had to remind herself that Brad wasn't Travis. "Sorry."

"I think you'd like it better if we weren't in traffic. Riding down an open highway is like nothing in this world." He reached up to tuck her hair behind her ear, the way he'd done when she'd been a teenager—after he'd tugged it playfully, that was. Heat swept over her. Her body hadn't forgotten the sensation, even if her mind had. His fingers scraped deliciously across her cheek as they withdrew, only to pause before retracing their steps.

He murmured, "I'll have to take you some time."

"Take me?" Chloe swallowed, her insides tightening in response to his touch.

"On my bike."

Her face went red hot. Oh, Lord. Why was she suddenly ascribing all kinds of motives to his words?

Because she could still remember what it was like to have her arms around his waist, hear his low, gruff voice piped directly in her ear, feel the vibrations from the engine rumbling through her entire body...

Yeah, she'd be up for that again, despite all her lectures to herself to the contrary. "I'd like that."

"Would you?" Was it her imagination or had his eyes darkened? "How about one day this weekend?"

"I work Saturday, but I'm off on Sunday." She couldn't believe she was actually considering going. A thought hit her. "You weren't thinking of going home to Connecticut, were you?" That was the last place she wanted to be right now.

"No. I was thinking about heading upstate and spending the day."

"At your parents' house?" The last she'd heard, they'd moved away to somewhere in New York State. The relationship between him and his parents had always been strained, to say the least, but maybe that had changed over the years.

His hand dropped back to his side. "No."

That one word told her the way nothing else could that she'd been wrong. Brad's feelings towards them hadn't changed. Although from what Jason had told her about them, she couldn't blame him.

"So what's upstate, then?"

"Nothing. It's just not the city." He paused for a minute. "It feels good to get away sometimes."

That was surprising as well. Not that he needed to get away but that he wanted her to go with him. She was sure he had plenty of women clamoring for the chance to be his traveling companion. Yet he'd chosen her.

She gave an internal eye roll. This was getting ridiculous. *First you think he's saying he wants to have sex with you on his bike—which is probably physically impossible. Then you delude yourself into thinking he wants to spend time with you in a romantic setting. Grow up, Chloe!*

He was only offering to take her because he had to. He felt responsible for her, the way he had as a teenager when he'd made sure she'd got home safely. Just what she wanted. To be a burden.

She sighed. "You don't have to take care of me, you know. I've lived a lot of years on my own."

"And you shouldn't have. Travis should have…" His voice trailed away. "Let's just say I want to show you what you've been missing."

Her mind took off running in another dangerous direction. What she'd been missing?

As if realizing how his words had come across, he clarified, "I was talking about New York."

"Oh." She seemed to deflate all at once. Of course he'd been talking about the state itself. What else would he have been talking about? Sex? Again?

She needed to realize once and for all that Brad didn't see her that way. And it was unlikely that would ever change.

CHAPTER EIGHT

"I WANT YOU to be careful around Dr. Coleman."

Reclining on a blanket in the park, half-asleep in the warmth of the sun, Chloe wasn't sure she'd heard Brad correctly. She half sat up, resting her weight on her elbows. "I beg your pardon?"

"You talked about learning how to…flirt." It seemed like he'd had to push that word out between clenched teeth. "He's not the man to try that with."

A quick flutter of something went through her, similar to the one she'd felt on the trip over. Brad had been right. Riding through the countryside on his motorcycle had been nothing like riding in city traffic. It had been exhilarating.

"And why is that?"

He lifted his wineglass to his lips and observed her for a second. "I don't want to see you get hurt again. And I think he's capable of doing just that."

Chloe disagreed, but didn't say anything. "So who would be a safer choice? You?"

"No."

The abrupt word took her aback. "Really? Why not?" The words were out before she could stop them. Did she really want to know the answer?

"I don't flirt."

Wow. "Ever?"

"Not the harmless stuff you're talking about. When I'm interested in a woman, she knows it. And she knows exactly where I want it to lead."

A shiver went over her as she pictured those mirrors in his room. She assumed he wasn't talking about marriage.

What would it be like to have a man like Brad put the moves on her? The closest she'd ever gotten had been at her wedding. And she'd just about convinced herself that those events had been fabricated by an overactive imagination. "So you can't be friendly with a woman unless you plan on sleeping with her?"

"'Can't' is not the word I'd choose." Brad set his empty wineglass next to the box of food. "Let's just say I'm not interested in wasting time playing games."

Playing games? Stung, she snapped, "Forget I said anything. I think I'll take my chances with Cade."

He dragged a hand through his hair. "Dammit, Chloe. Haven't you heard a thing I've said?"

"Yes. I heard you say you don't flirt, so I'm back to where I started."

His eyes narrowed. "You want to play games? Fine. Tell me what you have in mind."

In all honesty, she wanted to know why she wasn't worth his time. Did she want to wind up in bed with him—which was what he'd implied would happen if he showed his interest? No. But just for once she wanted to know what it would be like to have someone as dangerous as Brad pursue her with the intention of capturing her.

She shrugged. "I just don't want to make a fool out of myself, that's all."

"With Coleman?"

"With anyone."

"Okay, you've got a captive audience. So give it your best shot."

"Right now?"

A slow smile curved his lips, and he leaned forward and drew his thumb along her cheekbone. "Right here, Chloe. Right now."

Liquid heat ignited along the trail he'd left on her skin, and she could scarcely believe what she was hearing. Was he serious? She kept perfectly still as his touch continued to assault her senses, afraid that if she reacted she'd scare him off. She didn't know exactly why he was willing to make an exception, but she was going to grab it with both hands. Because if she didn't, she'd be back where she'd been when this had started: alone, with no hope of that ever changing.

"So where do you want to start?" What the hell had possessed him to agree to be her flirt buddy? Oh, he knew exactly what it was. Her veiled threat to involve Coleman. And the idea that Coleman would want her to be an altogether different kind of buddy.

His thoughts darkened. He'd told her the truth. He wasn't into the light-hearted back-and-forth quips that seemed to go on for weeks while he waited for some vague green light that allowed him to move to the next stage. No, when he wanted sex, he chose a woman who was just as interested in getting to the point as he was. He had no desire to climb on the emotional roller-coaster that went along with relationships. Or to be trapped in a box with no way out.

Sex was sex and nothing more.

He instinctively knew the act meant much more to Chloe, though. It was the reason she'd saved that part of herself for marriage. And look what she'd gotten in exchange. Heartache and a man who'd had no qualms about taking what she'd offered and then tossing it aside when he was done.

Isn't that what you do with women?

No. It was the reason he didn't play around with innocents

like Chloe. And why he didn't want Coleman to either. She wasn't a love 'em and leave 'em type of woman.

She'd stuck with Travis for six years, even though Jason said things had been bad for quite a while. For crying out loud, she hadn't even been willing to get on the back of his motorcycle after he'd passed the last of his medical exams because she'd been afraid Travis might get the wrong idea. Oh, she hadn't said it, but he'd seen the truth in her face. In the way the glow had faded from those beautiful baby blues.

So why was he allowing her to push him into doing this? He was not the right person for this particular job. He wasn't accustomed to holding back when he wanted something.

And if he decided he wanted Chloe?

Not a chance. He was a big boy. He could do this with his eyes closed.

He propped himself on an elbow next to her and raised his brows. "So, let's say we're out on a date, and you wanted to let me know you're interested. What would you do?" The image of her in that negligee passed briefly behind his eyelids. He chased it away with a muttered oath. She shrugged, staring down at the blanket.

He tilted her chin, forcing her to look at him. "This was your idea. Having second thoughts?"

"I don't want you to make fun of me."

"I've never felt less like laughing in my life." On the contrary, a sick sense of anticipation was building inside him that he couldn't will away as easily as he would have liked.

This girl was his best friend's sister, for God's sake.

"How will I know if I'm even doing it right?"

"I think I'll be able to tell." If the way his body had responded to having her behind him on the motorcycle was any indication, he wasn't totally immune to her, despite his assertions to the contrary.

She moistened her lips, the soft bottom one glistening. "I

think I'd rather just ask you questions and have you answer them."

Even easier. "Okay. Fire away."

"So…" Her voice dropped almost to a whisper and she hesitated for a second or two. "If you were here on a picnic with one of your dates, what would she do to hold your interest?"

One of his dates? He'd probably be sliding her panties down her thighs right about now.

Why did this game suddenly seem a little too dangerous?

And why was he all too eager to keep playing?

"Well…" He thought for a moment, trying to come up with something halfway chaste. "She might turn towards me so we were facing each other."

There. See? Easy. He'd give her a couple of quick tips and they'd be on their way home.

Instead of nodding her head and continuing with her questions, Chloe shifted to the side until she was resting on one elbow just like he was. The position made the dip of her waist and the curve of her hip stand out in sharp relief. He couldn't stop his eyes from following the line.

"Kind of like this?" she asked.

"Exactly like that."

"Okay. What else?"

His body quickened. Hell, she'd wanted to know if it was working. A little too well, and she wasn't even trying. And if she did?

Things could get out of hand. He should put a stop to this now, before she realized what she was doing to him. He was curious, though, to see how far she was willing to carry this little charade. He decided to push her. Maybe he could even scare her back into her shell.

"Well, she might sweep the hair off my forehead as she listens to me talk." His voice seemed to be affected by the tightening of his throat, coming out a little rougher than he intended. That could work to his benefit, though.

Chloe seemed totally oblivious, however. She reached out and did as he suggested, sliding her fingers deep into his hair, lingering when she should have withdrawn. "You used to tug my hair all the time when I was a kid, remember?" At his nod, she ran her fingers through it again. "Yours is softer than I thought it would be."

"Is it?" The tight sensation in his throat began to spread, reaching his chest, crawling along his abdomen and beyond. And she seemed to have no idea. Not good.

"This is really helping," she murmured. "Thank you for agreeing."

Yes. Thank you. His mind wasn't nearly as happy as the rest of him was. It was currently kicking his ass from here to across the sea.

"Tell me what else I would do."

As if he were a puppet—and he knew exactly what was pulling the strings, and it wasn't his head—he kept digging a deeper hole. "Well, *I* might move a little closer." He proceeded to do exactly that, sliding to within a few inches of where she lay. "Then I might stroke the side of her face, down her neck until I reached her shoulder." His hand followed the route in time with his words.

As he touched her shoulder—he wasn't even sure he'd applied any pressure to it at all—she lay back on the blanket, her eyes staring up at him. Waiting to see what was next on the agenda.

God help him, the words just seemed to keep coming. "Then…I might kiss her. Like this."

With that, his head began its fatal descent, until his lips touched hers.

CHAPTER NINE

A BUTTERFLY'S WINGS.

That's what Brad's lips felt like as they brushed across hers once, twice, three times. The sensation was intoxicatingly gentle, barely there at all. She'd never been kissed like this in her life.

She wanted to open her mouth, to drag him closer and really feel his mouth against hers, but she was too busy reveling in this luscious new world—one she'd never known existed.

Until this very moment.

A strange sound came up from her throat, a cross between a whimper and a groan. A quiet plea for more? Whatever it was, it changed the dynamic between them. His whole body came to a complete standstill for several seconds before coming back to life. He went down on his forearms, her breasts flattening as he settled over her. Warm hands moved to either side of her face and held it still.

That was when she realized that not only had she moaned against his mouth, she was straining upwards as well, hoping to increase the pressure. Brad seemed determined to keep to the original pace, his weight physically keeping her from speeding things up.

And that torturous, traitorous kiss…

Not plundering. Not invading. Just a sweet, steady touch designed to drive her insane.

His name wound around in her brain, seeking an exit that didn't exist.

Brad left her mouth, his lips brushing along her jaw in a long, slow journey that made her shiver with longing, made her insides coil tight in anticipation.

Oh, Lord, what was happening to her? The world was moving too fast and too slow, she was too hot...too cold.

Nothing was the way she'd expected it to be. The way it had always been.

"This is what I'd do." Warm breath slid along her ear carrying words she strained to catch. "I'd kiss her. Until she couldn't breathe. Couldn't think."

She was already there. So there.

But before she had a chance to respond he was gone, cranking his body upright and dragging a hand through his hair, while she lay stunned, her breath coming in short, desperate spurts.

He gave a hard laugh, his eyes staring down into hers, pupils as black as she'd ever seen them. "See? That's why I don't do flirting. It doesn't take much."

Her sluggish brain struggled to process the words.

It didn't take much to what? Turn her into a churning cauldron of need?

Oh, God. Was that what that was? He'd sensed what was happening with her—had been forced to back off before she reached for him with greedy hands? Before the light flirting she'd asked for suddenly turned to something much more serious?

He'd done exactly what *she'd* set out to do to Travis in that hotel room in New York City: seduce her.

And, unlike her failure with her ex, Brad had succeeded far too well. All it had taken had been one small touch.

Armed with a fresh cup of coffee, Chloe made her way across the street. She needed to get away for a little while and the tall shade trees of Central Park had beckoned her from the fourth-floor hospital windows all morning long. It was already warm but temperatures hadn't yet rocketed enough to cause the horse-drawn carriages to stop operating, though they might later on.

She sat on one of the benches that lined the street and gave a sigh of relief. Maybe the constant drone of city sounds would help drown out the cacophony in her head. Her fingers went to her lips as the events of this past weekend swept over her again. Unlike her thoughts, no amount of noise was going to erase the sensation of Brad's mouth on hers. Something that had followed her into her dreams, disrupting her sleep and making her feel edgy and irritable.

She hadn't seen Brad since their arrival at the hospital that morning, and for that she was glad. So much for not letting things get awkward. That kiss had shot that plan to hell.

Not only was there no more flirting going on, there wasn't much talking either. Well, except for shop talk. They could chat about patients and treatments until the wee hours of the morning and never hit on anything more personal than the glucose counts of such and such a patient.

Cade Coleman, on the other hand, had drifted in and out of the nurses' station today without a care in the world, giving her a friendly wink from time to time. Hopefully Brad wouldn't catch him and think she was practicing on the surgeon again. There was already some kind of growing tension between the men, and she didn't want to do anything to make the situation worse.

Taking a sip of coffee, she leaned back against the bench, taking in the constant flow of cars. This world was so different from the one she'd left behind in Connecticut. Everything was bigger. The buildings. The traffic jams and construction. Even Central Park itself had seemed to stretch on for ever when she'd looked down on it from the upper floors of the hospital.

Instead of making her long for the familiarity of her county hospital, the movement and activity here seemed to energize her, making her feel alive in a way she hadn't felt for a very long time. Maybe some of that was due to being free of Travis. But she wondered if it wasn't the city itself.

Her cellphone went off. Glancing at the readout, she saw it was the hospital.

"Chloe Jenkins here."

"Where are you?"

Brad's voice. Impersonal. Brusque. Just like it had been ever since they'd come back from the picnic.

"Central Park. Why?"

"We've got a TTTS. Can you get back here?"

TTTS... Her brain flashed through the acronym. Twin to twin transfusion syndrome.

"Stage?" she asked.

"Three."

Not good.

Although fairly rare, TTTS was restricted to identical twins who shared a placenta. One fetus's blood was shunted to the other, endangering not only the donor twin but also the recipient, if it progressed past a certain point. "On my way."

Dumping her empty paper cup into a nearby trash can, she stayed on the phone as she hurried to the corner to wait for the light to change. A million questions came into her mind. "Did her OB/GYN do an amnio reduction on the recipient twin?"

Brad's voice came back through. "Yes, but the problem is still progressing. Coleman wants to do a laser ablation."

Wow. If Cade wanted to destroy the blood vessels linking the two babies, things had to be serious. "When?"

"They're trying to schedule it immediately, which is why I need you back here. The nurses' station will be short-staffed otherwise."

She would have liked the opportunity to watch the procedure—as Angel's was one of the few hospitals in the U.S. that offered it—but she was here to help however she could.

The light changed, and she jogged across the crosswalk. "I should be there in about five minutes."

"Okay. See you when you get here."

Had she imagined the relief in Brad's voice? Of course she had.

As the doors of the hospital swished open a couple of minutes later, and the rush of cool air from the interior hit her, she smiled at the ordered chaos that met her eyes. A pink-haired clown—whose eight-foot height could only be the result of stilts—was busy swaying to some kind of rap music, his real smile almost as wide as the one painted on his face. His reflection gleamed in the mirrors and the polished floors. About ten delighted children had gathered around him, clapping in time to the beat.

It was easy to forget she worked in a children's hospital as the tiny patients on the fourth floor were still cocooned in their mothers, dependent on skilled doctors for their very lives. But here on the ground floor everyone was equal, doctors and patients alike.

A wave from across the foyer caught her attention. Layla, holding the hand of a young cancer patient, who, despite the patchy hair and pale delicate skin, was laughing. Layla put an arm protectively around her small charge as she smiled at Chloe, making an imaginary phone with her free hand and holding it up to her ear. *"Call me,"* she mouthed.

Chloe smiled back and gave her a thumbs-up. It was good to have a friend. Especially now.

The elevator gave a soft ping as it arrived on the fourth floor, but as soon as she stepped out she saw Ginny at the nurses' station, along with two other nurses. Where was the shortage Brad had talked about?

Maybe they hadn't gone to prepare yet. Although they didn't

normally pull nurses from the floor to assist. That job fell to the surgical nurses.

Brad appeared round the corner with Cade, the two of them in deep conversation.

Well, at least they were being civil to one another. They both spotted her at the same time, Brad frowning while Cade called out a greeting. "I understand you're going to observe the procedure."

She was? Her eyes went to Brad for confirmation as they drew near. "We don't get very many of these and I thought you might be interested." His voice had softened a bit.

How on earth had he guessed something like that? And why lie about his reason for wanting her to come back? Had he thought she wouldn't show if he told her?

Cade said his goodbyes, saying he needed to go scrub for the upcoming surgery.

Brad glanced down at her with a raised brow. "When I couldn't find you, I thought something might have happened." Before she could ask what he meant, he continued, "Something like Travis showing up."

Ah, that explained it. Even so, she couldn't stop the little jump in her stomach that he'd cared enough to keep track of where she was—had been afraid she might need to be rescued.

She did. But only from herself, evidently.

"Are you really going to let me observe?"

"If you want to." He nodded in the direction Cade had gone. "I had to give him a reason for calling you out of the blue."

The jump in her stomach turned into a pogo stick, bouncing between happiness with Brad and irritation with herself.

"I'd love to watch."

"Okay. I'd planned on observing as well, so I'll take you up. We can grab some coffee on the way." He started toward the elevators. "I hope I didn't disturb anything by calling you."

"Nope. Just sitting across the street on a bench."

He nodded. "I've been known to do that myself from time to time."

He had? Something in her wondered if he might have sat on the same bench she had. The thought caused that crazy pogo stick to land squarely on the happiness side of the equation.

"I've already had coffee," she said. "I probably shouldn't have another cup."

"We'll go straight up, then."

The ride in the elevator seemed to take for ever this time. Chloe strained to find something to talk about. "How's the mother handling the news?"

He scrubbed a hand along his jaw. "She'd already armed herself with information, so she knew this was a possibility."

"No, I mean how's she *handling* it?"

His hand fell to his side and he smiled. "You always were a softie."

"Yeah? Well, someone has to be."

"Mom is hanging in there. I think her husband is more scared than she is." He tweaked her hair. "And I always knew your soft outer layer hid a will of iron."

If only he knew. That iron core she'd once possessed was now pitted with rust and corrosion. One more hard kick and it would fall apart completely. Which was why she had to be careful with Brad. That kiss had taken its toll on her.

Was still taking its toll.

Brad would never knowingly hurt her, though. Not if he could help it.

But what if he couldn't? What if she, despite all her best efforts, turned out to be her own worst enemy?

CHAPTER TEN

A MOVIE THEATER without the popcorn.

The thought went through Chloe's mind as Brad guided her to the first row of seats in the observation room. Angel's was a teaching hospital so it stood to reason that there would be a room like this one, but she was surprised by how big it was, the transparent glass in front of them stretching from side to side like a giant screen.

No one else was in there but them at the moment, and Chloe found herself torn between wishing others would join them and hoping they wouldn't.

"Can they hear us?"

"Only if I turn on the system. It would be distracting to the surgeon if he could hear everything that went on in this room."

The words bought things to mind that made a wave of heat wash up Chloe's neck and collect behind her cheeks. Surely he'd never—

"The glass is two-way, though. We can see out and they can see in."

Was he setting her mind at ease or giving her a subtle warning not to get any ideas about practicing her flirting?

No fear of that. Her soul still showed the scorch marks from the last episode. Brad was way out of her league. While he could brush off that kiss and never think about it again, she was having some serious problems putting that chapter behind her.

What had she been thinking to suggest it in the first place? All Brad had to do was look at her sideways, and her heart started thumping like a jackrabbit's back leg when danger was near.

Like it was doing this very moment.

Cade entered the surgical area, where the patient and anesthesiologist were already waiting. He glanced up and nodded towards them. Chloe felt a strange kind of detachment looking down at the scene, almost as if she were having an out-of-body experience and was actually standing on the surgical floor.

But she wasn't. She was here with Brad.

If only she could detach from him as easily.

"Does the patient know other people could be watching this?"

He nodded. "It's disclosed in the admissions paperwork."

"I can't help feeling like a peeping Tom sitting here, though."

Brad leaned closer and their shoulders bumped. "It's the best way for surgical residents to hear and see exactly what goes on during surgery. They can observe how the team works together, learn new techniques or how to manage any complications should they arise."

It made sense, and it wasn't like the patient saw a crowd of people staring down at her. It just seemed intrusive somehow.

But so much less so now as Brad's shoulder was still touching hers. A steady stream of warmth seemed to be flowing from that connection, traveling down the length of her arm, settling in her belly.

Cade's voice came through the speakers, causing her to jump. "Are we ready?" He glanced at each person in turn and received an affirmation.

Soon caught up in what was happening, Chloe kept her eyes glued to the monitor to her left as it provided a better view than actually looking down at the floor. "Ablation of the shared blood vessels is done laproscopically?"

"It's safer that way. No reason to make a large incision in the uterus in this case."

It was almost like watching a movie with a running commentary. She just hoped there were no twists involved in this particular storyline, and that things ran smoothly.

Cade introduced the fetoscope into the opening, feeding it through the hollow tube until he reached the blood vessels in question. She could now see the rich red vessels that were starving one twin and oversupplying the other. "Getting ready to close the vessels."

A couple of quick bursts later, Cade proclaimed the ablation a success. The only thing left to do was drain some of the excess amniotic fluid from the recipient twin's sac. Then they'd close the small incisions. Chloe only realized she'd grabbed Brad's hand and squeezed hard when she felt his other one cover their joined fingers.

"Sorry." Her words came out on a half-laugh. "I guess I got caught up in what was happening."

She let go, and Brad gave his hand a shake or two. "It's okay. I don't use it much anyway."

"Surely you've had worse things done to you?"

"Surely." He was still smiling, but his tone wasn't quite as light as it had been a minute ago.

She glanced back down at the room below to avoid looking at him. "Will both twins survive?"

"That's the hope. We should know within the next couple of days."

Minutes later, Cade exited the room, snapping off his gloves as he pushed through the door. "The hospital's lucky to have him on staff."

Brad's mouth tightened. "That's what they tell me."

"Don't you like him?"

"He's good at his job. I don't have to like him." He glanced at her. "And what about you? Do you like him?"

Chloe shrugged. "I don't really know him. The other nurses seem to think he's attractive, though."

There was a pause then Brad stared through the viewing window at the people still working around the patient, cleaning up the site and getting ready to transport her to a recovery room. "I'll bet they do."

She couldn't tell if the words were sarcastic or if he was merely agreeing with her. "I think you two are a lot alike."

That got his attention. "You think so?"

"I do."

His eyes searched hers. "And what about your ex? Am I a lot like him as well?"

A few seconds went by before she answered him.

"No. You're nothing like him."

His fingers came out and stroked her jaw and he decided her skin felt just as soft and silky as it had the day of the picnic. "Don't be too sure of that."

He saw her swallow then her gaze went back to the floor. "Believe me, you're not. He cheated on me. More than once."

He cheated on me. Brad's eyes closed as myriad emotions churned to life in his gut—outrage, anger, along with a sudden realization. "You found him with someone else the night you showed up at my apartment."

"Yes." The tip of her tongue moistened her lips, and she opened her mouth like she wanted to say something else but clamped it shut again.

However bad he might be, Brad thought, he'd never cheated on anyone he was with. He kept his relationships clean and simple. Only one woman at a time. One short-lived fling after another. "What else did he do?"

Chloe's eyes skipped away again. "Besides cheat? Isn't that enough?"

"More than enough." He studied her face, trying to see past the pink cheeks and averted eyes. "But there's something else.

Something to do with this whole flirting business. Did he say you were unattractive?"

Her teeth came down on her lower lip. "No."

He waited, sensing there was something inside her fighting to come out.

"He said I was…frigid."

Brad wasn't sure what he'd expected her to say but that hadn't been it. He kept his voice very even, trying to push past the growing fury in his chest. "Excuse me?"

"W-well, *he* didn't say it. The woman he was with did. Said he was right about me…that I even looked frigid." She took a gulping breath and for a second he was afraid she might burst into tears. "I wanted to talk to someone about it, but it's just so…so…" her eyes went back to the floor "…humiliating."

He damned the man, putting his fingers under her chin and forcing her to watch him say the words. "It's not true, Chloe."

"It is true. I was standing right there when she said it." Her blue eyes flashed at him.

"I didn't mean they didn't say it. I meant that whatever that man said about you is a lie." He remembered the sexy way her body had arched in an effort to capture his mouth as they'd kissed. What had made it even hotter had been that she'd seemed totally unaware of how crazy she'd driven him, doing that. How close he'd been to giving in to his baser urges.

There had been an eager innocence about her that he'd never encountered before. It had taken him by surprise at the time, but now he understood. If he had been furious at Travis before, that emotion now paled beside what he was currently feeling. Whatever had gone wrong between them in the bedroom had been Travis's fault, and not Chloe's. He would bet his life on it.

His fingers tightened their hold. "Listen to me. You are a sexy, beautiful, desirable woman."

And he didn't trust himself not to throw her down on the floor and show her exactly how desirable she was.

"Then why didn't he want me?" Her chin trembled. "And why did I dread being with him?"

Because the man you saved yourself for was a bastard who stole everything from his beautiful wife and gave nothing in return.

"Travis cheated you in more ways than one. If I could, Chloe, I'd…"

Show you just how good it could be.

He wanted to say the words. They were on the tip of his tongue, fighting to get out. And it was true. He wanted to take her home tonight and lay her down on his bed and tease her mouth open. Taste her. Fill her. Take her to heights she'd never dreamed of.

But Jason's words clanged in his head, stopping his thoughts in their tracks with a warning that Brad had better not hurt her.

As if sensing the war going on inside him, Chloe's lips parted. "You'd what, Brad?"

CHAPTER ELEVEN

You'd what?

She repeated the question silently as she finished up Melanie Roberts's discharge instructions, glad that the woman—and her unborn baby—had recovered well from the surgery to repair the neural tube defect. Sending up a quick prayer that Cade's fingers had worked their magic, she stood up and made her way over to the patient's room.

More problematic had been the way her heart had leapt into her throat yesterday as she'd asked Brad what he meant. She could have sworn he'd been about to say something else entirely. Instead, he'd muttered something about kicking someone's ass, and then he'd gotten up from his seat, saying he needed to get back to work.

And that had been that. They'd both gone their separate ways and then had ridden back to the apartment on his bike. Only instead of his low, rich voice filling her head and her senses through the helmet speaker, she'd been met by silence.

She'd finally spoken directly with Jason, though, and had let him know that she was filing for divorce. She gave him the name of the attorney, and Jason had said their father would give the office a call and make sure all Chloe's bases were covered.

Entering the hospital room with her clipboard, she smiled at Melanie. "Are you ready to get out of here?"

"Absolutely." She laughed. "No offense to the chef."

"Believe me, we all feel the same way about that particular chef. He does make an excellent strawberry gelatin, though. Have you tried it?"

Melanie smiled. "Only for breakfast, lunch, and dinner."

"It never gets old, does it?" Chloe said, her hands going to her chest as she swayed back and forth as if in love. She smiled again and handed the clipboard to the other woman, showing her where to sign and going over some care instructions with her.

"I really have to stay in bed for that long?"

"Really. Your little one has to heal, and so do you." She squeezed Melanie's shoulder. "It'll all be worth it. You'll see."

"I know." Melanie scribbled her name just as a wheelchair manned by a cheerful hospital volunteer rolled through the door.

Taking the paperwork, Chloe helped her patient get into the wheelchair. "I think your husband is bringing the car round."

"He is. Thanks again for everything."

On impulse, Chloe bent down and gave the woman's shoulders a quick hug. "I want to see pictures when he's born, okay?" As she said it, she realized she might not even be here in three months' time. A pang went through her. After only a week she was already getting attached to the hospital and its patients.

And maybe a little too attached to her boss?

As long as he didn't notice, and she took care not to let things get too cozy, her secret should be safe. Although when they had been in that observation room, she could have sworn he'd been about to say something about men and women, and how he wanted to...

The huge expanse of mirrors over his bed came to mind just as the elevator doors opened, allowing Melanie and the volunteer to get in. As the wheelchair turned to face the front, her patient gave a happy wave. Chloe waved back, mortified to even be thinking about things like mirrors and Brad's naked muscular back.

Her eyes strayed longingly to the patient's abdomen just as the doors swished closed, cutting it off from view. Maybe someday *she* would be that pregnant lady. When she found someone who would love her as she was.

Even if she wasn't a firecracker in the bedroom.

Brad's words about her being desirable had given her a jolt of hope that maybe all was not lost. If she could find someone patient enough to show her the way, she'd make sure she held onto that person and never let go.

Or, if for ever was too much to ask, maybe he could at least teach her what love—real love—was.

Something smelled delicious.

Brad closed the front door to the apartment, trying to erase the image of a desperate father on his knees in the hospital chapel, begging God to spare his wife. God had. But the couple had lost their unborn baby—and with it the possibility of ever having another one. When the man's red eyes had met his in the doorway, he'd known without Brad saying a word.

"My wife?"

"She's in Recovery. She sent me to find you. I promised I would."

Brad had taken that promise to heart and had gone searching for the man in person. He'd known instinctively where he'd find him.

He'd lost patients before, wasn't sure why this was so different. Maybe because of the way that husband had looked at his wife, as if no love had ever been greater. He hadn't left her side until she'd been wheeled away for the surgery that would change both their lives.

"Chloe?" he called, shaking free of the memories.

The scent of cooking grew stronger as he tossed his keys and wallet onto the table in the foyer of the apartment and headed for the kitchen. Relief and irritation warred for first place. Relief that she was here, and irritation that she hadn't waited for him before hopping on the subway and heading home. He'd gone looking for her once his patient had been stabilized, and had been told she'd already left for the day.

Without saying a word to him.

He needed to get over this nagging worry that Travis would come looking for her. She was an adult, she didn't need him to be a babysitter. Besides, he'd already seen what could happen between them if he got too close. Chloe needed someone who would handle her with kid gloves. That someone was not him. Maybe he'd make a visit to Katrina's to get whatever was going on with him out of his system.

The idea filled him with distaste, which in turn made his frustration grow.

"Chloe." He allowed his irritation to come to the fore as he called her again.

She popped her head around the arched doorway that led to the kitchen. "In here. I'm making us something to eat."

"Why?" The last thing he wanted was to have her cooking for him. When it was time for her to go, he wanted it to be a quick, clean break.

Her brow puckered. "I know you've had a hard day. I thought it was the least I could do, especially as you're letting me stay in your apartment. Consider it part of my rent."

"I already told you, you're helping me out of a jam at the hospital."

"I know." She hesitated, looking into his eyes. "I heard about your patient, Brad. I'm really sorry. Are you okay?"

His jaws clamped shut as he fought to stem the unwanted tide of emotion that rose inside him. He fought hard to give his unborn patients the best possible start in life. Something he hadn't had when he'd been a kid. And when things went wrong with any of his cases, it ate away at him.

He could rail at fate as much as he liked. But just like with the padlocks on the doors of his childhood home, he'd learned that begging and screaming didn't change a thing. Those locks had taught him at least one important survival skill, however. He was an expert at bolting the doors of his heart and keeping any unwanted emotion locked out of sight, and it got the job done. He'd learned to make choices based on what he knew about the world. Just like Chloe would have to do.

She disappeared again. He stood there wondering if he should just go to his room and try to shut out the day. It's what he wanted to do, but knew he'd end up feeling like a jerk if he did, because Chloe had gone to all the trouble of fixing him something to eat.

So he followed her.

"I'm making shrimp garlic alfredo. Hope that's okay. I remember you liked Mom's version of it."

He did, although he hadn't had it in years. Mrs. Jenkins had always remembered he liked it, too. Actually, though, he liked just about anything she cooked. And she made sure he knew he had an open invitation to their dinner table.

He'd taken her up on it time and time again when the front door at his parents' house had been locked tight, or when they'd left him to fend for himself while they had gone on various business trips.

"What can I do to help?" His body relaxed. He was damned glad Chloe wasn't like Katrina or another of his dates—who'd be going on and on about her newest shoe purchase or eying his apartment with a speculative gleam. Little did any of them know he didn't intend to marry. Ever.

He may have grown up in a household that seemed like every kid's dream home—no fighting, no chiding about childhood tantrums or, later, about broken curfews and less than stellar grades. There had been no harsh emotions at all. But beneath the surface things had not been how they'd appeared. The snick of a lock had preceded hours of unbroken silence. A silence that had been more menacing than anything he'd ever known.

The Jenkinses, on the other hand, had been open with their emotions and vocal as hell when someone had done something wrong. Ben Jenkins had chewed his butt up one side and down the other after his motorcycle accident. Threatened to take his bike to the junkyard if he ever pulled another stunt like that.

Wonder what the man would think about him taking his daughter for a ride on the back of that very same bike?

Chloe broke into his thoughts. "I think I've got it covered if you want to take a shower. Besides, this is the only apron I could find in the house." It took him a second to realize what she was talking about.

The apron had been in his house? A couple of women had cooked for him over the years, but it was normally breakfast. One of them had evidently expected to stick around.

A pang went through him. Had he hurt someone the way Chloe's ex had hurt her?

No, because he never made any promises. If anything, he cut relationships shorter for just that reason. Before that claustrophobic sensation of being trapped had time to set in. He didn't want anyone to get the wrong idea.

He took a step back, wondering what was with all his melancholy thoughts tonight. It had to be because of his patient. Something about the look on her husband's face when he'd realized his wife was still alive...was going to survive her ruptured uterus. He'd seemed to take on a glow that had transcended the sorrow of losing his unborn child. The man had taken one last look at the stained-glass cross then had closed his eyes as if sending up a quick thank-you prayer before he hurried from the room, leaving Brad alone.

He'd wandered over to one of the chairs and sat down, hands draped over the pew in front of him, realizing he'd never really visited the chapel before. But there was something peaceful about it, whether it was because of the décor or because of some spiritual presence, he didn't know. What he did know was that it had made him want to find Chloe.

Only she hadn't been there.

Instead, she was here, fixing him dinner.

He relaxed a little bit more. "I'll get changed."

"Good. I'll uncork the wine." She motioned to the bottle on the counter. One of his better bottles from the look of it, but what the hell?

He smiled for the first time that day. "I'll be back in a few minutes, then. Don't start without me."

"Absolutely not."

Evidently ten minutes was all the man needed to look and smell heavenly, because when she turned to check the cabinets for a tureen or something to put the pasta sauce in he was propped against the door frame, watching her. She let out a little squeak before she could stop it. "How long have you been standing there?"

"About a minute and a half."

Heat rushed up her face when she realized her gaze was trailing down his chest and had landed just below his belt buckle. "I, um…was just looking for a couple of bowls for the pasta and sauce."

His lips quirked as if he realized exactly what she'd been doing. "Well, by all means, let me help."

Without saying anything else, he opened cabinet doors until he found a couple of good-sized bowls.

His scent filled her head, making her feel slightly dizzy. She shook it in an effort to clear it. "I like your china pattern. I wouldn't have thought you were much for flowers, though."

The delicate gold rimming the plates and the pink roses were definitely not what she would have thought he'd pick out for himself. When he frowned, her thoughts froze. Had some past or present lover bought him dishes?

She swallowed. Not that it was any of her business but she'd already set the table with them as she hadn't been able to find any other plates in his cupboards.

He tilted one of the bowls as if seeing it for the first time. "My mother sent them as a house-warming gift."

"That was nice."

He gave a hard laugh. "You would think so, wouldn't you? My mom always knows just the right thing to say or do. She's a master at managing and meeting expectations—and instilling that trait in others. It's all about doing what's expected of you."

CHAPTER TWELVE

DID BRAD KNOW how bitter those words sounded?

Probably not. Her heart ached for him. Her own parents were so involved in their kids' lives—sometimes too involved—that she couldn't imagine what it would be like to have parents as detached at his parents had always seemed to be.

"People can change," she said. "Maybe your mom really was trying to be nice."

"I'm sure she was." The tight-lipped response told her he didn't buy her theory.

Maybe Brad was right. Chloe knew from experience that some people never did change.

Once everything was on the table, they ate in silence. Brad complimented the food but didn't seem to be in a hurry to start any kind of conversation. The silence eventually got to her. She cleared her throat. "How's the hunt for a new nurse coming? Have you had any applicants?"

"I had several interviews today, as a matter of fact."

"That's great."

So soon? Her heart plummeted, landing somewhere around her knees. She knew he was going to look for someone else. Knew she was due back at her old job in less than a week, but it wasn't easy hearing how painless it would be to replace her.

Why wouldn't it be? Travis had replaced her before she'd even officially left the marriage.

Besides, the sooner Brad got her out of the hospital and out of his hair, the sooner he could go back to his old, free-wheeling lifestyle. Who knew? Katrina might even stroll back into the picture as soon as the coast was clear.

She swallowed, trying to blot out the wave of self-pity that sloshed through her stomach. Chloe Jenkins: invisible and most certainly expendable.

Getting up from the table, she picked up her plate and headed for the safety of the kitchen, thanking the dinner gods that she'd finished eating because there was no way she'd be able to force down one more bite. The cheesecake in the re-frigerator was going to have to wait.

She heard the scrape of Brad's chair and tensed in front of the sink. He came in and laid his hands on her shoulders. "You okay?"

"Just fine. There's cheesecake in the fridge if you want dessert."

"I'm good." He turned her to face him. "What's wrong?"

"Nothing." She was so desperate to avoid his gaze that she threw out the first thing she could think of. "Do you want another glass of wine?"

He searched her face. "Let's take the bottle into the living room and sit for a while. You can tell me about your day."

Uh…he already knew everything about her day because they worked together. She saw almost exactly the same patients as he did. But right now she was more than grateful for an excuse to slide away from him. And one more glass of wine wouldn't do her in.

Whiskey, however… Yeah, she didn't want a repeat of her first night at the apartment. She'd drink a second glass and then retreat to her room or the kitchen. She could always say she needed to do the dishes.

"I'll get the table and the dishes later on. Just leave everything where it is."

Had the man read her mind? She sure hoped not, because there were things inside her head she did *not* want him to find.

Picking up her glass as Brad retrieved the bottle of wine along with his own wineglass, they made their way to the living room. Chloe was reminded of that fateful first time she'd sat here—how horrified she'd been at what she'd been wearing beneath her coat.

That seemed like a lifetime ago. Maybe it was. What had seemed like the closing of a chapter was more like the final page of a book. The new one, full of crisp white pages, was just waiting for the right opening line. Only she had no idea what that sentence would be.

Chloe sat on the brown leather sofa, glad when he didn't choose to sit in front of her on the ottoman again. Instead, he settled in the space beside her and lifted the bottle of wine to fill her glass. She dutifully held it out and watched the clear liquid trickle until it hit the halfway point. He did the same with his own then set the bottle on a side table.

As there was no way he simply wanted to talk about her day, she wondered if he was trying to find a tactful way to get her out of his apartment. She decided to take the bull by the horns.

"Did you have any luck with the interviews?"

He leaned back against the cushions, his right arm sliding along the top of it. She swore she felt the tip of her ponytail move in the process. "None. So I've been doing some thinking."

"You have?"

He gave a soft laugh. "As surprising as that may seem to you, I do think from time to time."

This time the bobbing of her ponytail was not her imagination. What was he doing back there?

The continued subtle tugging on her hair was beginning to give her that weird quivery feeling in her stomach again. She cleared her throat in an attempt to take her mind off it, hoping he'd start talking again. "And what have you been thinking about?"

In a casual move he propped his left ankle on his right knee and shifted his body to face her. "How attached are you to your current job?"

Oh, God. He *was* trying to get rid of her. Wanted to make sure she wasn't going to cause a scene when he found her replacement. "Don't worry, I'm not desperate for a job. I already have one, remember?"

"So you wouldn't be interested in staying at Angel's on a more permanent basis?"

"I'm not sure what you mean." She thought she'd just made it clear that she wasn't angling for the position.

"Aren't you?"

Bewildered, she shook her head.

The subtle brush of something soft across the nape of her neck made her swallow. The warmth in her stomach increased. He was trailing the tip of her ponytail across her skin, and her gaze somehow landed on his mouth before she yanked it back up to his eyes. Was he trying to drive her crazy?

"Would you stay at Angel's, if I asked you to?"

Her thoughts moved slowly, as if slogging their way through thick molasses. "You want me to stay?"

"I thought I'd made that obvious at the beginning of the conversation."

"No—I thought. I thought you were trying to tell me not to get too comfortable." She licked her lips. "Are you offering me the position?"

His mouth curved in that slow, devastating smile that wreaked havoc on her senses. "That depends. Would you say yes?"

She wanted to, heaven knew. But something about the way he said it—along with that damned sweep of hair across her neck—made alarm bells go off in her head.

"Did Jason put you up to this?"

"Jason? No, of course not." His smile faded.

She gulped. She could only think of one other possibility. "Are you doing it because you think it's expected?"

The sudden darkening of his eyes told her she'd made a serious gaffe. The prickly sensation on her nape halted. He'd just talked about his mother giving him a set of dishes because it was the expected thing to do. Equating his actions with hers was not a good thing.

"Is that what you think of me, Chloe?"

"No, of course not. I didn't mean— I know you're actually…"

"Actually what?"

"A nice person." Something else she'd said about his mother's gift. Wow, she was really hitting them out of the park this evening.

He laughed, the hand in her hair tightening, forcing her to look at him. "I'm really not, Chloe. Just ask your brother. I think he might know me better than I know myself."

The pounding in her chest couldn't be her heart, could it? Because she could barely believe he was offering her the perfect way to leave her old life behind. And although she wanted to grab it before he changed his mind, she had to be sure he really wanted her to stay.

"Why do you want me here?" She touched his hand. "And please don't tell me it's because you feel sorry for me. I—I couldn't bear it."

Swish. Her hair brushed the side of her neck this time, sliding under her chin, along her jaw. Her breath caught in her throat.

"You're good at your job. The patients and the staff all like you. And I know I can work with you." Another tug on her hair. "So please don't compare me with my mother."

"Sorry about that." She smiled. "Jason told me what you had to deal with."

His head tilted. "And what was that?"

Uh-oh. "He didn't gossip about you, Brad. He just came home so angry one day I thought he was going to explode."

"Angry at me?"

"No. At your parents." She paused. "I pulled him into the backyard and pestered him until he finally let it slip."

"Let what slip?"

"That your parents had padlocks on…" She swallowed. "That they used to lock you out of the house sometimes." The words sounded horrific when said out loud, and Chloe immediately wished she could call them back.

She wasn't about to admit what else she knew. That a teenage Brad—as tough and cynical as the best of them—had fought back tears as he'd told Jason what he'd endured. His parents hadn't merely locked him out of the house—that had been during his later years. But when he'd been younger, his mother had routinely locked him in a closet in his bedroom whenever he'd done something she hadn't liked. Jason had seen one of the locks and asked about them.

Brad hadn't understood why his parents hadn't loved him the way Chloe and Jason's parents loved their kids. The way they loved *him*.

His motorcycle accident had happened a mere week after his confession. Chloe was pretty sure it hadn't been a coincidence. She could remember her terror when she'd seen the damage to his face, his shredded T-shirt…bleeding arm.

Brad had gone very still at her words. Well, most of him, anyway. One small muscle in his cheek was tensing and releasing in a slow, methodical movement that held her captive. Made her mouth go dry.

For a second she thought he was going to withdraw his offer and get up and leave, but he didn't. He sat there, without saying a word, until that muscle finally went still. "I don't want to talk about my parents."

"Okay." She pulled in a breath, relief going through her. She was just as desperate to change the subject as he was. "What do you want to talk about?"

Her ponytail, which had gone slack over the last couple of minutes, went taut again with a couple of quick bumps, and she realized he'd wrapped it around his hand. He used it to tip her head back an inch or two.

"I don't want to talk at all."

The pupils in his eyes grew, turning black. With anger?

Maybe. But Brad wouldn't hurt her. She knew that without a doubt. "What do you want to do, then?"

"Something your brother warned me not to."

Panic started to skitter up her spine, coming face to face with a warm, lethargic wave of need that was traveling down it. The two battled for control of her central nervous system while her vocal cords acted of their own accord. "And what is that?"

"This." Brad's pupils swam before her eyes, until they came so close she could no longer see them. Then his mouth covered hers in a searing kiss.

CHAPTER THIRTEEN

SHE EXPECTED TO feel fear. There was none.

A man was using her hair to hold her prisoner—the way Travis used to do. Was devouring her mouth like he couldn't get enough of her, and all she felt was elation.

That couldn't be right.

Neither could the way her lips were pressing closer, parting to actually invite him in of their own accord instead of clamping shut to prevent the unwanted invasions of the past.

Because this was different.

Brad may have kissed her to shut her up, but she hadn't realized until now how desperately she'd wanted to repeat that day at the park.

There was no mistaking this for flirtation, though. This kiss was all business. And she couldn't get enough of it.

A small sound exited her throat. Her eyelids slammed shut as the whirling emotions caught her up in a funnel cloud, sweeping her along some unknown path. He let go of her ponytail, his hands going to either side of her face, thumbs lining the hollows beneath her cheekbones.

His tongue took her up on her invitation and she tensed for a second as it slid past her lips, but despite the desperation she sensed in his kiss he didn't hurt her. Didn't force his way in and cut the tender insides of her mouth with his teeth.

This was exploratory. Feeling his way. Brushing along her tongue. Licking the roof of her mouth. The backs of her teeth.

Some instinct had her tightening around him, forming a channel that guided him, squeezed him. Coaxed him to stroke her.

A low groan met her ears as he did just that.

He liked it.

Brad hadn't said a word. Hadn't given her a blow-by-blow list of instructions on what he wanted her to do. And yet—as his hand moved to cup the back of her neck and the friction of his tongue across hers set her on fire—she knew.

Her arms wound around his neck, grateful just to let herself feel for once—not have to do something someone else wanted.

Yet somehow she was. The confusion of it all tangled up inside her, but she let it. She could try to unravel it later. But right now…

Umm…

His lips left hers and trailed along her cheek, kissing each of her eyelids. She wanted him back where he'd been. Hadn't finished kissing him yet. But even as she lifted her head to find his mouth again, he stayed on track with whatever he was doing. Kissing the tip of her nose. Her chin. Nudging it up so he could slide beneath it.

Okay, so she could kiss him again later. Because what he was doing right now was…was…

Fantastic.

The heat of his mouth continued down her throat then roamed back up the side of it until he reached her ear. And bit it gently.

A shiver went over her, the air rushing from her lungs in an audible sigh.

She wanted him everywhere at once. As soon as he left one place, she missed him. But, then, so did the next place he visited. Until she was a squirming mass of need, her whole body crying out for more.

Her nipples tightened, and instead of recoiling at the thought of his touch they were seething with anticipation.

She moved closer, frustrated at the angles that kept her from pressing fully against him.

As if he'd read her mind, he eased her down onto the wide couch until her head sank into the softness of the overstuffed arm.

Then they were body to body, one of his legs between hers, the hard ridge against her right thigh unmistakable.

She waited for the fear to finally make its way into the pit of her stomach, but his mouth was back at her ear. Whispering this time.

"You okay?"

The words took her by surprise. Made tears spring to her eyes.

Not once had Travis ever asked her that. Not even afterwards.

She nodded, her lips touching his face, then following the same path he'd taken on hers. But before she could complete the trip, he'd captured them with his own, his hand on the side of her neck, thumb stroking her throat as he kissed her.

These kisses were more familiar. The same light brushes she'd experienced at the park.

That wasn't enough this time. She wanted more. Wanted that same hard kiss he'd given her a few minutes ago. But when she tried to increase the pressure, he pulled back with a soft laugh. "Your husband was a fool."

She stiffened, coming back to herself all at once. All the reasons why this was a bad idea flooded her. But when she tried to scoot away, he held her in place. She opened her eyes and found him watching her in a way that made her squirm.

He brushed a strand of hair from her forehead. "I want you,

Chloe, but I don't want you to do something you're going to regret."

Regret? The only thing she regretted was that she was going to have to tell him the truth. That *he* was the one who'd end up with a pile of regrets if this went any further, not her.

"I'm not very…" Her throat closed up, and she had to fight to get the words out. "I can't…. I don't want you to be…"

Disappointed.

He cupped her face. "I won't be. Even if it goes no further than this."

Surely that wasn't the truth. But as she continued to look at him, she saw nothing but raw sincerity reflected back at her. How could that be? He was still hard against her leg. His breathing not quite steady. Would he really be okay if she called a halt to it right here?

Something inside her said he would.

She took a deep breath. "I want it to."

His fingertips brushed her cheek. "You want it to what?"

"Go further than this."

His eyes darkened. "Are you sure?"

"If you promise not to…" How could she put it into words? She didn't honestly think he'd make fun of her afterwards, but she didn't want him to get part way into it and then realize she was so not what he was hoping for. "I want to try. But I don't know if I can."

"Chloe, look at me."

She thought she had been. But she found the center of his pupil and focused.

There was an intensity swirling inside it she hadn't noticed before.

"The second you start to feel differently, I want you to tell me, and we'll stop."

She wouldn't tell him. She never did.

His fingers tightened on her shoulder. "Promise me."

And admit she was a failure? Again? She shook her head.

To her surprise, Brad sat up, dragging a hand through his hair and swearing softly under his breath.

She caught his hand before he could get up and walk away. "Please don't go."

"I don't want to hurt you."

"You won't." Did she really believe that? That the act itself wouldn't hurt? No. But even if there was some kind of physical discomfort, she knew that he would never wound her deep down inside, where it really mattered.

"Then promise me."

"I—I… It's too embarrassing." She averted her eyes.

"You don't have to use words. If you don't like something I'm doing, hold onto me like this…" he gripped her arms "… and push. That'll be my signal to back off. It's that easy. And I'll be okay with it. I promise."

"Are you sure?"

"Have I ever broken a promise to you?"

"No."

He leaned down and kissed her lips. "Okay. Your turn. Promise me."

She waited long seconds before she got up the nerve to say it. "I promise."

At her words Brad released the tension that had been steadily building in his jaw. He wanted this woman more than he'd ever wanted anyone in his life. And he'd just promised to stop the second she gave his arms a little squeeze. He hoped to hell he actually could. It had taken almost every ounce of his strength to sit up when she'd shaken her head and refused to agree to his terms. But he'd found the willpower then, and he would find it again if it came down to it. But right now all he wanted to do was kiss that beautiful mouth all over again.

The second his lips lingered on hers, a sigh rippled through her chest as if she'd been waiting her whole life for this. The thought inflamed him, made him want to take her in a rush, but he pushed the need aside and instead savored the way she returned his kisses, reveled in the tiny sounds she made when he lifted his head to move somewhere else. How could any man in his right mind call her frigid?

Chloe was anything but.

Instead, there was an untapped innocence about her that he'd never thought he'd find sexy—until now. *Virgins need not apply* had always been his motto.

He didn't need the headaches or the complications. But this was something very different. And he found himself wanting to break all his self-made rules to have her.

Just this once.

Chloe wasn't looking for another husband. And he certainly wasn't looking for anything lasting either.

Maybe he was as untouched as Chloe was, in some ways. And that thought made him tighten all over again.

Her hands on his shoulders pulled him back to her, until they were breast to chest. He eased away just long enough to recline beside her again, then wrapped his arms around her, burying his face in her neck and breathing her scent deep into his lungs. When her head shifted slightly once or twice, he leaned back and frowned, then realized her ponytail was pressing against the cushions.

That couldn't be comfortable. "Let me get that."

He tilted her head to the side, finding the elastic and sliding the loops—one at a time—over the length of hair. His fingers pushed into the thick, glossy strands and set them free. "Better?"

"Yes." She licked her lips. "Do you want to go into the bedroom?"

He did. Wanted to see her sprawled on that huge bed for a reason other than sleep, wanted to watch as she straddled him and took him deep inside. But something made him hesitate. That refusal to promise to make him stop.

Had she done that before? Let Travis do things she didn't want to do without attempting to stop him?

He nuzzled her cheek, his decision made. "Let's stay here for a while."

He was going to make this all about Chloe. Show her that all men were not created equal. Some really did care about their partner's enjoyment. Show her how much it enhanced his own pleasure to know she was responding to his touch. To his murmured words.

He could wait. For ever, if necessary. But he had a feeling Chloe had already been kept waiting far too long.

CHAPTER FOURTEEN

IT BURNED.

His touch. His lips. His body—even through his clothes. And Chloe was slowly going up in flames.

She'd never gotten this far before without tensing, without dreading what she knew was coming next. But Brad's fingers had edged beneath the hem of her shirt with care, sliding over the bare skin of her stomach until she found herself arching toward him rather than cringing away inside. He'd spent what had seemed like hours just getting to this point. As if there were nowhere else he'd rather be.

Lips touched her. Skated over her collarbone just as his hand covered her left breast, using the barest amount of friction. She pushed into his palm, asking silently for more. He responded with an equal amount of pressure in return.

He was right. She didn't need words.

And neither did he, evidently. His actions spoke volumes.

He cared about how she felt. About what she wanted. Something about that was freeing. Made her realize that Travis had been all wrong about her. She *was* able to respond. Just not to him.

Chloe pulled in a deep breath to increase the contact, wanting something but not sure what it was. When he kissed the corner of her mouth and stayed there while he trapped her nipple between his fingertips, a whimper erupted from her throat.

That's what she'd wanted. He'd known.

His breath released on a shaky note. "You're driving me crazy, you know."

She was driving him crazy? He didn't know the half of it. She was so far over the edge she wasn't sure she'd ever be able to make it back in one piece.

Turning her head, she captured his mouth, letting him know the feeling was mutual. He deepened the kiss, his tongue finding hers and coaxing it to follow his, until she found herself where she'd never thought she'd be. He tasted of wine and all things male, and she slid her tongue in a little bit further. He rewarded her by stroking the pad of his thumb across her imprisoned nipple.

The pleasure intensified, along with her desire to take things to the next level. She'd never craved the male and female joining the way she did now. It reminded her of the expectations she'd had when she'd been young and naïve. Before they'd been shattered by reality.

But Brad was making her hope all over again.

Even through her bra the pleasure had been intense, but the second he pushed the fabric aside and the contact was flesh against flesh, she grabbed hold of his arms, hanging on for dear life.

Brad froze, and she wasn't sure what was wrong for a second then remembered their signal. He really would stop.

The second she asked.

Instead of pushing him away, she pulled him closer, her arms going around his back, one hand brave enough to slide over the curve of his butt and press her thigh against the bulge of flesh.

"Slow, Chloe."

His words said one thing but his body said something else. She hadn't had to touch him to get him hard. In fact, it seemed to be the other way around. The more he stroked and kissed her, the more aroused he seemed to get.

And suddenly she didn't want slow.

To illustrate that point, she allowed her hand to trail around to the front of his body, her fingers tracing his length, only to have him stop her.

Heat crawled up her face as remembered humiliation curled around her throat, strangling her. She never seemed to get it right.

"What's wrong?" His whispered words just made it worse.

"I don't know what you want."

"Don't you? I want you."

The words were simple enough, but if he did, why didn't he want her to…?

"If you touch me, Chloe. I'm done for." He paused. "Just let me love you."

The pained smile told her exactly what he meant, and it had nothing to do with her being inept but the opposite. He wanted her so badly that one wrong move on her part could make him come unglued.

For the next fifteen minutes he proceeded to show her with his lips, with his tongue what she'd never realized she'd been missing out on over the years. By the time his fingers finally tunneled beneath the elastic waistband of her scrubs, and then beneath that of her panties, she was shaking with anticipation. Would he rip them off her and take her in a rush?

She wanted him to. Badly.

But he didn't. Instead, his fingers found her. She wasn't even horrified to realize she was slick. All she felt was wonder when he lazily explored every inch of her, moistening his fingers and sliding them over the most sensitive spot on her body.

The world stopped turning as the focus narrowed, zooming in over and over again until everything centered over that one point in the universe. His thumb continued to stroke over her while his middle finger slid inside her without the slightest hint of resistance.

Amazing.

That word was a blip on a radar screen that appeared for less than a second before it was joined by other, crazier words, all heading for the center. *Want. Need. Take.*

Between the rhythmic stroking, both inside and outside her body, the fire that had been growing steadily higher suddenly flared out of control.

Things melded into a single point of focus: Brad's ragged breathing at her ear, the rise and fall of her hips as she asked for—then demanded—more from him, the way he increased the tempo and pressure in response.

She strained upwards as everything came together at once. And the inferno suddenly reached for her and consumed her alive.

Some distant part of her consciousness heard his murmured "It's okay. I've got you. I've got you" as she came undone all around him.

Several seconds went by before those blue eyes focused on him again, and she drew a deep shuddery breath and let it out again. "Whew. I, uh…I'm not sure I've… Is it always like this?"

As hard as it was for him to concentrate on her words right now, he leaned down to nuzzle the bottom of her chin and tried. "Always like what?"

"I've never done *that* with a man."

His head came back up. *That?* Since she was married he was pretty sure she'd had sex before, unless Travis was crazier than he'd thought. So that meant… "You've never had an orgasm with a man?"

Her cheeks flamed, and she shook her head.

He swore under his breath. She'd said Travis had cheated, that he'd called her frigid, but surely he'd tried to warm her up before he'd entered her. If not… Sudden anger flared in his chest. That was his signal to stop right here.

"I think you've had enough for one night." He forced a smile to take the sting out of the words, thankful they both still had their clothes on.

"No! I mean, what about you?" Her thigh brushed against his still aching flesh, causing him to grit his teeth. "You haven't…"

"No." And it looked like tonight was going to be a very long night.

"Please, Brad. I want to. I *need* to." Her throat moved. "Just to know once and for all."

He wasn't sure what she meant, but he was going to have to move away from her. Soon. "Know what?"

"If there really is something wrong with me."

He said I was frigid.

His fingers tightened their hold on her. Travis Maroni deserved to have a couple of important items lopped off.

He smoothed the hair back from her face and kissed her mouth. "There's absolutely nothing wrong with you. I think we just proved that."

"But you don't want to finish it."

If she only knew. "I *do* want to." He nudged his flesh against her to prove his point. "I'm just not geared towards…" He had been about to say "being gentle" and then hesitated. The women he'd been with were as sexually aggressive as he was, for the most part. He'd never felt the need for anything else.

But having this conversation was doing crazy things to his body—he found himself wanting what he'd never wanted before. And it was contrary to what his body was clamoring for him to do: bury himself inside her as hard and as fast as he could, and to hell with the consequences.

She leaned up and kissed his chin, her fingers touching his face. "Then take me to bed. Please."

He was damned if he did…and damned if he didn't. Because if he refused, she'd see that as proof that Travis was right. But if he carried her off, there was no guarantee he was going to be able to hold off long enough to prove her biggest fear was baseless.

"Please."

That whispered plea was his undoing. He rose to his feet and scooped her up, pausing to place a long, hard kiss on her lips. Her response was instantaneous, her arms going around his neck, opening to let him in.

You're going to live to regret this, Davis.

Since when had that ever stopped him? Striding to his bedroom, bypassing the switch to the overhead light, he laid her down on the bed and then flicked on the bedside lamp. He sat down beside her and helped her take off her shirt and then shimmy out of her scrubs, leaving her panties and bra in place.

"You're sure?" he asked.

"Yes."

He slid his fingers into her hair and kissed her again, then stood, staring at her as he unbuttoned his shirt and shrugged out of it. Her lips were still soft and swollen from his earlier kisses, her clothing askew, hair wild and untamed as it spilled over his pillow.

His pillow. All the thoughts that had spun through his head the night of her wedding came back as if it had been only yesterday.

She blinked up at him, her gaze sliding over his chest, before moving to where his fingers were undoing the buckle to his belt.

"If you don't like something, same rules apply," he said. "I want to know."

He shoved down his pants and his briefs, then kicked them to the side, watching as she assessed him, heard the quick huff of air as she breathed.

"What?" he asked.

Her eyes came up to meet his, and he saw the first hint of panic. "You're bigger than he is."

And exactly why did he get the feeling that was a bad thing?

Obviously, not only had Travis not waited for her fulfillment before taking his own, he'd evidently hurt her as well.

He moved to the end table and took out a packet, throwing it on the bed. "It'll be okay, Chloe. Trust me."

"I do." She lay back. "Tell me what you want me to do."

He smiled and hooked his fingers beneath her panties and yanked them down her legs. "Nothing. Absolutely nothing."

When he'd said "nothing", he hadn't been kidding. Brad kept her breathless with a steady stream of kisses. His tongue mimicked the sex act, varying the rate and timing of his thrusts until she was moaning into his mouth, her hands trying to force his head even closer.

Then his warm hand slid over her belly and teased her thighs apart, one finger sliding effortlessly inside her before she had time to tense up. It moved deeper, taking up the same rhythm as his tongue.

Oh!

His palm hit the most sensitive place on her body at the exact moment his tongue and finger were at their deepest. It repeated with each and every stroke. Her body went wild with want. Climbing rapidly.

Oh, God, she was going to lose it all over again. Before he'd had a chance to…

But, no, he was moving over her body, his weight settling heavily between her legs, so she couldn't clamp them shut. This time she did tense.

"Shh." His voice was at her ear, the low rumble coming out almost pained. "Relax. I won't hurt you. Promise."

Promise.

She could still grab his arms, and he'd stop. He'd promised he would.

They wrapped around his back instead. He wouldn't hurt her.

His teeth nibbled across her jaw just as she felt him pause outside her entrance. She gulped as he dipped just inside then withdrew. Nice and easy. He repeated the action and her body seemed to draw him in a bit further, her hips rising to meet him this time.

It didn't hurt. He hadn't slammed into her like she'd expected—like she was used to. And instead of burning friction, she felt the smooth, steady glide of his body against hers.

She licked her lips and used the pressure of her hands on his back to ask for a little more. He gave it.

Further this time.

Two more strokes and he was all the way inside her, and the sensation was...

Heavenly. Stretching, full, but in a good way. Such a good way.

She lifted her hips again, and Brad matched her movement for movement. His hand slid between their bodies and found her again, coaxing her with his touch.

"Watch me, Chloe," he whispered, his teeth nipping the joint between her shoulder and her neck, wringing another moan from her throat.

Her lids parted, and she realized they'd been screwed shut since the moment he'd lain beside her on the bed. And since his lips were still against her neck, still torturing her with slow sensual love bites, her eyes were drawn to the expanse of mirrors above her head and the breath whooshed from her lungs.

What she felt, she could now see. The room was dim enough that their bodies didn't stand out in stark relief. Instead the play of light and shadow held her captive.

Brad's muscular haunches were tensing and releasing with

each thrust, his elbows resting on either side of her shoulders. The double dose of sight and sensation was intoxicating. She saw everything. The teeth digging into her bottom lip, the arch of her neck as his mouth dragged inch by inch along her shoulder, punctuating each kiss with a bite.

Thrust...release. Thrust...release.

She lifted her hips faster, harder, still watching the ghostly reflections above her. Brad's fingers, which had been gently stroking the sensitized flesh between her legs, suddenly moved, trapping the nub between his thumb and forefinger, his head lifting to stare at her with an intensity that was frightening as his fingers echoed the pumping going on in other places. Her body went wild, and she bucked against him, desperation pouring over her in waves.

Hurry. Hurry. Hurry. Hurr—

Chloe screamed as it hit her.

"Yes!" The word hissed across her cheek as Brad went impossibly deep and planted himself there, the contractions inside her intensifying until she wondered if she could ever make it back from such a place.

The only coherent thought she could capture was that he had been right. It didn't hurt.

CHAPTER FIFTEEN

JASON WAS GOING to skin him alive.

Glancing at the ceiling, the evidence of all he'd done was right next to him curled in a ball, her hip pressed against his side, his arm stretched along her thigh. The tattoo on his shoulder tingled, remembering her lips trailing over it the previous night. He brought his hand up to scrub away the sensation.

A thin sheet was all that covered her nakedness, much like the coat she'd worn that first night.

That sheet hadn't been anywhere around when he'd finally carried her to his bed. It was as if he'd unleashed something wild and elemental in Chloe, her second orgasm creating an explosion that had engulfed them both within seconds.

Is it always like this? Her words had gutted him. Made him take her when he should have simply given her release and then set her free.

If Jason was out for blood, Brad knew exactly whose he should start with.

Against his will, he stroked her leg as he continued to stare at her in the overhead mirror. Soft hair, mussed and tangled from his fingers. Warm body that had welcomed him home not once but twice last night.

He swallowed as his flesh tightened all over again at the memory of what they'd done together. Chloe had straddled him, just like in his earlier fantasies, but not at his insistence.

She'd taken the lead that second time, hesitating only a second or two when he'd winced, his struggle to hang on becoming a physical effort that had rivaled anything he'd ever done.

When she'd frowned and asked him if he was okay, he had only been able to groan an affirmation at the gorgeous creature who'd become a siren of the worst sort, leading him to his doom as surely as those ancient sailors had been.

The question was, what did he do about her?

He couldn't bring himself to regret what they'd done because Chloe had needed to discover the truth about good sex. And it had been good. Too good. The temptation was there to keep taking what she offered. To drink his fill and then move on, just like he always did.

Just as he always would.

He shifted his body to the side and wrapped his arm around her, drawing her against him. For now he would just enjoy the feel of her body, the scent of her skin. And then he'd try to forget any of this had ever happened.

"Chloe, that's abuse." The concern in Layla's eyes was evident even beneath the shadowy canopy of trees in the park. "Tell me you're not going back to him."

Chloe wondered if she'd made a mistake telling her new friend about Travis, but she'd had to talk to someone. And when Layla had mentioned wanting to get out of the hospital for a while, carrying their coffee cups to Central Park had seemed like the obvious solution.

Layla motioned to the park bench, and Chloe gladly parked herself on it.

She took a careful sip of her coffee. "I'm not going back. But it's a little more complicated than that."

"More complicated than your husband humiliating you in bed, and then…cheating on you?" There was a strange hesitation in those last three words, as if Layla had had to push them out from somewhere deep inside her.

Should she tell her friend the extent of it? May as well. She'd already told her the worst part.

Because it was.

The night with Brad had been fabulous, wrenching a re-action from deep within her soul. One she'd never dreamed possible.

It made her realize Layla's words were true. Not only had Travis been all about taking everything for himself during their encounters, he'd done things during the act that had hurt her physically—nothing overt but subtle things that she now wondered if he'd done on purpose. Maybe punishing her for not doing exactly what he wanted.

Brad, on the other hand... She closed her eyes and sighed. Was she setting herself up for heartache of a different sort?

"I slept with Brad last night."

"Brad?" Layla's mouth popped open. "Brad Davis? *Our* Brad Davis?"

Okay, so hearing it put in those terms wasn't the most reas-suring thing in the world.

Chloe nodded. "So technically *I've* cheated on Travis as well."

A hand covered hers. "Oh, honey. You're talking apples and oranges here. You've filed for divorce, right?"

"I've talked to a lawyer. He's drawing up the paperwork. The sooner this is over, the better."

"Good." A jogger went past, and they both waited until he was some distance away before either spoke. "Is it awkward, seeing Brad at work?"

"You have no idea."

He'd already been up and out of bed when she'd awoken this morning. Neither of them had said anything about what had happened, and Chloe had been glad. She'd wolfed down the bacon and eggs Brad had made, surprised by how hungry she was. And also by how energized her body felt. She was sore, but it was a good soreness. Brad had brought her to completion each time before giving in to his own needs. Were all men except Travis like that?

"Oh, I think I do." Layla's soft words pulled her from her thoughts. For a panicky moment she thought her friend was saying that she'd slept with Brad as well, but there'd been no hint of anything between them when he'd asked Layla to show her around the hospital.

"I don't understand?"

Layla leaned back and crossed her legs, brushing an imaginary speck of dust from her navy pants. "Alex Rodriguez."

"What about him?"

When the other woman turned toward her, her nose crinkling, Chloe got the message. "Oh. You two…"

"A long time ago." There was a long pause. "I was married to someone else at the time."

So she hadn't just pretended to know what Chloe was going through. She'd been through something similar.

"So are you and Alex still together?" Chloe had never seen the legendary neurosurgeon in person, but there was a kind of awe that hung in the air whenever his name was mentioned.

"No. After I left LA, I never thought I'd see him again. I didn't even realize he was at Angel's until the day of my interview."

"How awful." She put her arm around Layla's shoulders and gave her a quick squeeze.

"It has been." Layla smiled. "It feels so good to be able to tell someone about it."

Chloe thought for a minute. The last thing she wanted to do was go home and face Brad after what had happened the night before. And it sounded like Layla could use some downtime as well. "Why don't we go out tonight after work? Just us girls?

There's a tapas bar in the meatpacking district that's supposed to be great. We can grab a bite to eat and drown our sorrows."

As long as she stuck to frozen daiquiris, rather than straight whiskey, she should be fine.

"I'd love that. What time do you get off?"

"Six."

"Great. Do you want to meet in the lobby?"

"Sounds good."

Layla took one last sip of her coffee then crumpled her cup. "So...how was it?"

"How was what?"

Her friend's brows went up, and she gave her a pointed smile. "The sex. With Brad."

Draining her own coffee cup, Chloe climbed to her feet, her cheeks heating. "It was...amazing."

CHAPTER SIXTEEN

CHLOE CRACKED OPEN another peanut and popped it into her mouth.

The noise in the tapas bar was unbelievable, especially for a Thursday night. She and Layla had to almost yell to be heard. But it was just as well. Her own churning thoughts seemed to leach away into the chaos that surrounded them. It did feel good to get away for a while, which brought up another point. If she was going to stay in New York, she was going to need to get her own place.

That was, if Brad still wanted her to stay.

Why wouldn't he? He'd been with Katrina after all and had still expected to work with the woman afterwards. Was this any different?

No. She could be just as much of a grown-up as Brad. No more of this idealistic naivety she'd carried around with her for the last six years. Travis may not have knocked it completely out of her, but the reality of the way Brad lived his life sure had. He seemed to have everything together and was perfectly happy. No wonder he'd laughed at her for wanting to hang onto her virginity until marriage. And he was right. What had it gotten her?

No, it was time to make some changes, starting now.

Layla's hand suddenly went to her wrist and squeezed. Blinking at her, Chloe saw her friend mouth, "Oh, God."

She followed Layla's gaze, and her own eyes widened. Brad had just walked through the door with another man.

Oh, no! She'd left a note on his desk, saying she was going out to dinner with a friend. She'd assumed he'd head home, although she had no idea why.

Her head suddenly pounded. What if he was here to pick up a woman? Ugh! Maybe she could crawl beneath a table and hide.

But if Chloe was horrified, Layla looked positively stricken, her face as pale as a ghost's. Looking back at the men, she realized why.

That had to be Alex.

The men were almost the same height with wide shoulders and powerful frames, but whereas Brad's hair was an inky black, the other man's was a shade or two lighter. Female heads followed their progress as they made their way deeper into the place, and just when Chloe hoped they'd head to the bar without noticing them, Brad's eyes swept the interior and found hers.

Oh, hell.

He bumped the other man's shoulder and nodded their way.

"Please, no." Even through sounds of clinking glasses and noisy conversations Layla's quiet plea came through loud and clear. But there was nothing to do but sit there and watch the nightmare unfold.

Of course the only available table when they'd first arrived had been one with four chairs. And the place was still packed. Any hope of scrambling away or slipping out the door was long gone. Even now, the two men headed toward them.

Brad stood behind one of the empty chairs. "I got your note and assumed you were headed for O'Malley's. I guess I assumed wrong."

O'Malley's was the hospital staff's go-to place for drinks after work. Was that why Brad had come here instead? Hoping to avoid her? Her heart contracted even more as Alex nodded towards Layla and said hello. Knowing what she did now, this had to be unbearably awkward for Layla. But she displayed none of the panic from a few minutes ago. Instead, her face was as cool as her smile, and she motioned to one of the chairs. "Do you want to sit?"

Brad glanced at her, one brow lifted in challenge. She gave a quick shrug. If he wanted to sit, who was she to stop him? He drew the chair a little closer, crowding her a bit. When his elbow touched her arm as he reached for the peanut bowl, she froze, a quick shiver running through her.

The other man sat as well but, unlike Brad, he kept his distance from Layla. A waitress came over to take their order.

"I'll have a whiskey. Neat." Brad smiled at Chloe's frozen daiquiri. "I see you're going for the lighter stuff nowadays. Smart girl. Especially if you end up being our designated driver."

Was he making a reference to her behavior the last time she'd tried drinking straight whiskey?

"Drive your bike?" she said. "No thanks."

A slow smile went across his face. "But you don't mind taking a ride every once in a while."

Her face heated as Layla and Alex both turned to look at her. The question on Layla's face was as plain as day.

She ignored it and shifted her glance to the neurosurgeon, taking in his brooding eyes, wide shoulders, long fingers drumming on the table's Formica surface. The man was freaking gorgeous. No wonder Layla had fallen hard and fast for him all those years ago.

"So how did you two wind up in the meatpacking district?" Layla asked.

"We were trying to get away from the crowds," Alex said.

Layla's brows went up, and her lips twitched. "So were we."

Instead, Brad and Alex had found the two people who were trying to avoid this very meeting. And while she and Layla were having to work to be heard, the men's voices seemed to carry with ease, seemingly unaffected by the room's noise.

"Have you ordered dinner?" Brad's arm went to the back of her chair in a strangely proprietorial move that would have made her laugh under different circumstances. But now it just made her nervous. Did he think she was going to practice her flirting skills on Alex or something? And there was no way she would, even if she were tempted. Not after what Layla had told her.

"We ordered appetizers." She licked her lips. "We can share if you'd like."

Something touched the back of her blouse and she almost jumped out of her skin before she realized it was his thumb, stroking back and forth from its perch on the chair. She stared straight ahead, afraid that if she looked at him he'd flash that lazy smile at her that turned her words to gibberish and her insides to mush.

"I might share," he said. "Or I might want more of the same. It depends on what you're having."

More of the same?

Good heavens. Was he talking about food or their time under those mirrors? This man was out of her league in so many ways.

"I'm having sh-shrimp cocktail." Yep, even without looking at him she was having trouble getting her words out.

Layla spoke up. "I'm having nachos."

"Sounds good to me." Alex's eyes fastened on Layla's and the other woman went pink. If Chloe hadn't known better, she'd think there was still something between these two.

Thankfully, once the men's drinks arrived and the extra appetizers had been ordered, Alex and Brad proceeded to talk shop, trying to see who'd had the oddest cases over the years. Some of them made everyone at the table laugh, and some were just plain bizarre. When Cade's name came up later in the conversation Brad's mouth thinned as he asked how he'd come to be in New York.

Alex paused for a moment, before shaking his head. "I'll tell you about it later."

Layla caught her eye, the pediatrician's released breath puffing out her cheeks before she mouthed, *"Can you believe this?"*

Her thoughts exactly. Chloe's laugh changed to a cough when both men stopped to look at her.

"Something funny?" Brad asked.

"Oh, um, no." She glanced at her watch. Almost eleven. "I'm probably going to need to get back to the apartment, actually. I'm wiped."

Yeah, last night had been long. Followed by a day that had had her emotions swinging from high to low. She really was tired.

"Me too," said Layla.

Alex leaned back in his chair. "I'm going through your part of town. Can I give you a lift?"

Chloe saw the other woman's teeth come down on her lip, and she looked torn. Finally she shook her head. "No, I'm good. I'm going to catch a cab and head right to bed."

Alex's jaw tightened but he didn't argue. "Okay." He glanced at Chloe and Brad. "How about you two?"

"I've got my bike."

"Right." He tossed a couple of bills on the table and stood. "See you tomorrow?"

The words were directed at Layla, who nodded. "Tomorrow."

Giving Brad and Chloe a stiff nod, he headed out the door.

Layla's eyes followed his exit, making Chloe's heart ache for her friend. She reached over and caught her hand. "Are you sure you don't want me to go with you? I could even sleep over if you want."

Brad's mouth murmured close to her ear, "Scared?"

His words may have been lost in the din around them but she heard it loud and clear. And the answer was a great big yes.

"I'll be fine." Layla squeezed her hand. "Thanks, though. And for tonight. I had a good time."

So had Chloe, even after Brad and Alex's unexpected appearance. Or maybe it was because of it. Something she didn't want to spend too much time thinking about in case the answer wasn't one she wanted to face.

Because despite what had happened between them last night, her days of living with Brad would soon come to an end, as would his part in her life—just like it had when she'd gotten married. It wouldn't be any different just because they'd had sex. Brad had slept with lots of women and had walked away from all of them without a problem. She was just a face in a crowd.

Why, then, did the thought of becoming another discarded woman turn her soul to ice and her heart to lead?

CHAPTER SEVENTEEN

"YOU WANT ME to what?" Brad couldn't have heard her correctly.

Two days had passed since their fateful encounter. Followed by two nights of lying in bed. Alone. Knowing that the only thing separating them was a wall.

And a locked door. He hadn't forgotten about her asking for the key. He'd noted the one she'd left in the bathroom door as well.

Surely sleep deprivation had affected his eardrums, along with his mind. And hers. Because this morning she was standing in his hallway, already dressed in her work scrubs, asking if he would teach her about sex.

She shrugged, not quite meeting his eyes. "I— It's not a big deal, really. You *know* things."

The way she spoke said it *was* a big deal. At least to her.

"Things." Just having this discussion in calm rational tones seemed ludicrous somehow. Of course, Cade's smirking image chose that very moment to waltz across his thoughts, reminding him of the whole flirting incident. Exactly how far would Chloe go to learn about these so-called "things"? Or who would she ask if he refused?

Hell, what was he going to do? Jason had called him yesterday to check on Chloe, and Brad had been short with him on the phone. It was none of his damn business what his sister did, but he didn't want the wrath of the whole Jenkins clan coming down on his head either. "It's not for ever. Just until I find my own place."

He propped his shoulder against the door frame of his bedroom. "And just what kind of knowledge would this entail? Instructional or practical?"

Are you actually thinking about doing this, Davis? You've got to be out of your damned mind.

"Is there a difference?"

He crossed over to her, toying with the idea of scaring the living daylights out of her and making her see how dumb an idea this really was.

Only she'd planted the thought in his mind, and he couldn't seem to banish it. He could have her in his bed, whenever and however he wanted. No guilt. No worrying about going through the romantic little formalities like dating.

Better yet, he could hear those sexy little whimpers she made when he stroked down her throat, kissed the shadow of her breast.

And *that*, my dear Chloe, is how you make a man hard without even touching him.

"There's a big difference." He planted his hands on the wall on either side of her head and stared down at her. "Instructional involves this…" He touched a finger to her temple and drew tiny circles. "Head knowledge."

He moved in closer and slid his hands behind her until they'd curved over her delectable butt, pulling her tight against him. "Practical knowledge involves doing. Repeatedly."

"Oh." Wide blue eyes blinked up at him.

"Which will it be, Chloe?"

"P-practical."

He leaned his head down until his lips grazed her cheek, drawing them across until he reached her ear. "Good answer."

Hell, so much for scaring her. He'd just sealed the deal. Well, almost. There was just one more thing.

"We need some ground rules," he whispered, the scent of her filling him with something that had to be pure lust.

"Ground rules?" She seemed dazed, tilting her head closer to his mouth. Good. That's just how he wanted her. Off balance. Willing.

He gave a soft laugh. "Surely you don't think I'm going to agree to your crazy plan without thinking this through?"

"I suppose not. If you don't want to..."

"Oh, I want to. Make no mistake about that." One hand released her butt and found her ponytail and used it to tilt her head up. "And if I didn't have to be at work in less than half an hour. I'd show you exactly how much."

"Oh."

"Yeah. 'Oh.'" He bent down and planted a hard kiss on her mouth, which quickly spun out of control. The scent of the jasmine soap she'd put in his shower filled his lungs, and he sucked it down greedily. Yes, he was crazy. Was a fool for going along with this, but what the hell? He'd done all kinds of stupid things during his life and had lived to tell the tale.

Still kissing her, he pulled her closer, letting his body's reaction speak for itself. He needed her to know exactly what this meant. He was going to have her. Tonight.

And she'd see exactly the kind of practical knowledge he had in mind.

When he came up for air and looked down at her, he relished the way her clear blue eyes had darkened, the outer ring no longer distinguishable from the lighter center. It seemed she was serious about wanting this.

And he was shocked to find that he wanted it just as much as she did. He'd toyed with the idea of extending their time together, and she'd just given him all the ammunition he needed—had made it easy. Too easy. And that set a little warning bell off in the back of his mind. But for now he would ignore it. Chloe had come to him for help. And he wasn't about to turn her away.

"Are there still going to be ground rules?" Her voice had gone all breathy and feminine and hell if it didn't make him want her that much more.

"Definitely."

"Like what?"

"You'll sleep in my bed."

"Every night? Even when we're not…"

He nipped her lips. "Even then."

Why had he just made that a condition of their arrangement? *Practicality.* When he wanted her, he could just roll over and have her.

"What else?"

"No other men between lessons."

This time she frowned. "Of course not." She leaned her head back. "Were you planning on having other women?"

His brows contracted. Did she really think he would? "No."

His fingers closed over her hips, feeling a possessiveness that startled him. No, not possessiveness. It was protectiveness. It had to be. He didn't want her to wind up with another bastard like Travis.

Right. And that's exactly what he'd tell Jason: he was sleeping with his sister to protect her.

That was sure to get him a fist to the face…maybe two.

And would Jason be wrong? Probably not.

He let her go and took a step back, dragging a hand through his hair. Time to get real. "Are you sure about this?"

Chloe blinked at him then gave him a slow smile that made his stomach flip, made him want to reach for her all over again. "More than sure. I want you to teach me everything you know."

Teach me everything you know.

Chloe rolled her eyes as she adjusted the blood-pressure cuff on her next patient. Had she really said that to him?

That wasn't what she wanted. Not really. She'd had a husband who'd tried to teach her everything he knew, and it had been the worst six years of her life.

No, what she wanted was for Brad to teach her about her own body. Teach her how it felt to be loved. Really loved. Teach her how to ask for what she wanted.

She smiled as the blood-pressure cuff deflated on their twin-to-twin transfusion patient. "One twenty over seventy. That's ideal."

Sitting on a stool, she noted the woman's weight and other vital information. "So how are the babies doing?" Cade's nimble fingers seemed to have worked a miracle.

"My obstetrician thinks both twins have stabilized but wants me to meet with the surgeon to make sure everything's progressing well."

The words *"progressing well"* struck a nerve. Her own situation with Brad seemed to have turned some kind of corner, and she wasn't sure how she felt about it any more.

Immersing herself in her work seemed to be the only thing keeping her sane at the moment. The more patients she saw, the less chance she had to think about tonight. About what was going to happen. Brad had made it clear he wanted her. The sooner, the better.

It's what she wanted as well, right? Somehow, though, she'd expected him to balk at the idea. Or at least put up some kind of token argument. Instead, he'd dragged her against him with the talk of ground rules and wanting to start immediately.

He could have any number of women who were infinitely more experienced than she was. And yet he was agreeing to sleep with her in what she'd come to see as a cold-blooded arrangement that she'd been stupid to even suggest.

So why did he seem so eager?

She wasn't that beautiful. Men didn't swoon at the sight of her. So what was he getting out of it?

Maybe he pitied her. Was trying to help out the next poor sucker who got involved with her.

That explanation didn't seem to fit either, although that could just be because she was too mortified to think it might be true.

Swiveling her attention back to her patient, she nodded at the gown on the end of the bed. "Our fashion designer is dying for you to try out her latest creation. While you're getting dressed, I'll page Dr. Coleman and let him know you're here." She squeezed the woman's shoulder. "We're all pulling for those little ones."

"Thank you. They've got a lot of family and friends praying for them too."

"I'm glad." She picked up the chart and headed for the door. "See you in a few minutes."

Chloe went to the nurses' station to call Cade. Before she could do that, he appeared in the flesh. "Clara Serrano is here." She handed him the chart.

"Everything look okay with her?"

"Her vitals are all normal. She's feeling movement from at least one of the fetuses. Dr. Morris wants to see if the size ratio has changed at all."

"Sounds good. I'll take a look." He tapped the counter with the chart. "Have you seen Dr. Davis, by any chance?"

She had. Quite well, actually. But that's not what Cade was asking. "I haven't seen him since this morning." Not since he'd dropped her off at the hospital entrance and then revved up his bike and rounded the corner on his way to the parking garage. He hadn't touched her as she'd unsnapped her helmet and shaken her hair loose, but his smoldering look had spoken volumes. She was getting some tonight.

The thought made the corners of her lips curve much higher than they should have.

Cade evidently thought so too, because his brows went up

and he leaned his elbows on the desk, bringing him a little closer. "Very nice. Is that smile for me?"

"That's what I'd like to know." The low voice came from beside them, making Chloe jerk to attention and spin to face it.

Brad. And although his tone was calm and reasonable, his expression was anything but. Narrow-eyed, with lips in a tight hard line, he studied her face—from which her smile was now gone.

Cade, on the other hand, straightened. "Is it against hospital policy to comment on someone's pretty smile?"

"I'd prefer that you both do your jobs instead."

A thread of anger ran up her spine, replacing the warm anticipation of a few seconds ago. "I think we both were. If you'll excuse me, I'll go and check on one of my other patients."

She stalked toward the nearest room, having no idea which patient it belonged to. All she knew was that her irritation was out of proportion to the situation. But if Brad thought he could use their little agreement to his advantage at work, he was going to find out he was dead wrong.

A hand on her arm stopped her before she made it halfway to the door. She came to a halt, already knowing who it was but unable to bring herself to look at him. Not with the way her chin and everything inside her was trembling.

"Hey, hold up a second." He turned her round. "Sorry to step on your toes, but I don't trust the guy. Something's going on with him."

"He was just trying to be nice."

His gaze trailed over her face, stopping at her lips. "Maybe I'm afraid he'll make a move on you."

"And if he did? I'd think you'd be glad."

His palms slid down her arms, creases forming between his brows. "And why would you think that?"

"It's obvious, isn't it?" Her voice dropped to a whisper, not wanting anyone to hear what she was about to say. "Poor little Chloe needs a tutor. Who wants to be stuck with that kind of duty?"

Certainly not her ex, who'd made his exasperation plain.

The corners of Brad's eyes crinkled as he continued to look at her. "You make it sound like a death sentence."

Chloe shrugged. "You said it, not me."

There was a pause, then his fingertips stroked across her cheek. "You're a beautiful, sexy woman. Any red-blooded man would give his right arm to be in my position. Even Coleman. It's why I don't want him hanging around you."

"He's not hanging around me."

"Maybe he'd like to."

Chloe tried to decipher his meaning. "And that would bother you."

His eyes darkened, his smile fading. "Oh, yeah. It would bother me a whole lot. Because you're all mine. At least for now."

CHAPTER EIGHTEEN

THE BATHROOM DOOR wasn't locked.

As strange as she found his aversion to keys, in this instance it suited her purposes. Brad had said he was going to take a shower, and Chloe had stood there undecided. Her irritation about the scene at the hospital had faded, and anticipation had wormed its way back into her head.

Should she wait for him to get the ball rolling or try to hurry things along? Their last time together had been all about her—he'd seen to her every need. Maybe this time she could return the favor. After all, she knew the mechanics of it. And instead of waiting for Brad to ask for what he wanted—something she'd never had to worry about with Travis, because he *always* had—she could beat him to the punch.

Maybe this way she wouldn't feel like a receptacle—there to be used at someone else's convenience—like she had during her marriage.

She eased the door opened and slid inside, the dense moist fog from the shower enveloping her. The clean scent of shampoo filled her senses, and she relaxed, a smile working its way up from her chest.

Things were about to get interesting.

Pulling a towel off the rack beside the door, she padded over to the shower on bare feet and set the towel down on a nearby stool. She paused at the curved entryway that led to the interior of the stall and tried to plan her first move. Before she had a chance to do anything, a hand reached round the corner and snagged her wrist, hauling her through jets of water—which came at her from all angles—until she smacked into a bare, muscular chest.

She screeched as the warm spray continued to pelt her hair and her scrubs, plastering them to her body.

"What are you doing?" she spluttered. "How did you even know I was out there?"

"I have my ways." He reached around her and adjusted the spray until it was less cyclonic and more mist-like.

"You do? That sounds a little scary." She laughed to cover up the fact that she was only half kidding.

"Does it?" He leaned against the tiled wall and pulled her between his splayed legs, his already stiffening flesh pressing into her belly. He seemed unfazed by the fact that she still had all her clothes on. She, on the other hand, was aware of every inch of his nakedness.

"Yes," she whispered.

"It should." His hand slid into the wet locks of her hair and held her in place as he kissed her, before going to the bottom of her shirt, hauling it over her head and dropping it onto the black marble floor next to him.

She swallowed. Here it was, the test of her mettle. It was one thing to get carried away like they had on the couch a few nights ago and let things go further than she'd meant them to. It was another thing entirely to sneak into a bathroom intent on doing unto him as he had done unto her.

Only he'd turned the tables on her. Again.

Time to turn them back her way.

She took a step backwards, forcing herself to maintain eye contact as her fingers found her bra clasp and released it, feigning nonchalance as she tossed the garment on top of her shirt.

She was rewarded by the darkening of his pupils as they slid over what she'd revealed.

So far, so good.

The best part was that he wasn't directing her every move. She was free to go in whatever direction she chose.

And she chose this. Her thumbs hooked in the waistband of her scrubs and pushed them over her hips, then she stepped out of them. One corner of his mouth tilted, and when she chanced a glance down, she saw the spark of interest was holding steady. Okay, so it was more than a spark. Much, much more. The sight gave her a shot of confidence.

She could do this.

Measuring out another dose, her fingers plucked at the elastic band of her satin panties and she raised her eyebrows.

"Definitely." His voice had dropped to a low growl.

Her cheeks heated, but she slid the underwear down, his eyes following her progress. Once off, her toes curled around the garment and nudged it towards the growing stack of clothes.

Now they were both naked. Both equal.

His arms opened up. "Come here."

She moved back into the circle of his embrace and pressed her lips to his collarbone, adding a little bite like he'd done to her shoulder the last time they'd been together. A groan erupted from his chest when she moved over an inch and repeated the act, her tongue lapping over each spot. He tasted wonderful.

Brad's hands went to her shoulders, kneading and stroking, his eyes closed as she made her way down his chest, licking beads of water from a masculine nipple as she went. His breath hissed through his teeth, fingers tightening on her for an instant or two before relaxing their grip, thumbs stroking the sides of her neck.

Lord, her body was already pulsing down below, and he hadn't even touched her in any of those places yet. When he did…

She was going to go up in smoke.

Reaching his other nipple, she changed tactics, tightening her lips, her mouth tugging on it with slow, steady strokes.

"Hell, woman," he ground out, one hand moving to fist in her hair, though whether to urge her to continue or pull her away she wasn't sure…and didn't really care. Because she was already on the move. Down his abdomen, following a thin, fascinating trail of hair.

The muscles of her stomach turned inside out, clenching and releasing, a terrible excitement building deep inside her.

The moment of truth.

She went down on her knees, the water on the floor of the shower warm and wet. Just like his skin. Just like between her legs. Closing her eyes, she kissed his thigh, his arousal brushing intimately along the side of her cheek as she drew her tongue in a slow arc up to his hip.

The hand in her hair tightened fractionally, drawing her back toward the middle.

"I want your mouth," he whispered.

Chloe froze, familiar pressure crowding her chest, obstructing her throat.

She'd been planning to. And she wanted it. More than anything. She parted her lips and started to lean forward, but the past wouldn't release its grip on her airway. Her breath came in terrifying gusts, her lungs sucking down every drop of oxygen they could find. Fear began to paralyze her body, shutting down one muscle group after another.

Her lids squeezed together. "I can't." A half-sob came out. "I can't. I can't."

The second he let go of her hair, she lurched to her feet, forcing her legs to move.

Move, move, move.

She ran, her feet slipping once, before she regained her balance, her only goal: escape.

* * *

Brad caught her before she reached the door, damning himself to hell for his mistake. The second his arms wrapped around her waist, she broke into wrenching sobs that gutted him, branded him the worst kind of fiend. He'd been so caught up in the moment, in the exotic sensation of her lips brushing across his skin, that he'd forgotten she wasn't like the women he normally went after. And Chloe had paid the price.

"Shh." Still holding her, he lowered himself to the floor, ignoring the chill of the marble, until he had her cradled in his lap, her head pressed into his shoulder as she continued to cry. "It's okay. God, Chloe, I'm sorry. I never should have…" He closed his eyes, his throat working against the flow of emotions.

What had he been thinking? He'd known all along he was not the right man for this job. He'd just proved himself right.

He kissed the top of her head as her sobs slowed, tightening his grip to make sure she didn't try to run again, his hand stroking up and down her back. "Talk to me. Please."

"I wanted to…but Travis…" Her voice cracked between words.

Something from one of their earlier conversations came to mind. The whole talk of being frigid, the affairs with other women. "What did he do, Chloe?"

She shook her head, avoiding his gaze.

"Tell me." He forced his voice to remain soft, trying to coax it out of her.

"He m-made me do things."

He blinked then, as her meaning took hold, raw fury rose in his chest filling his head. "He forced you?"

Her head tilted back and watery eyes met his. "No, he didn't rape me. But he would tell me what he wanted, and then when I tried to do them…it hurt. Or…" she licked her lips "…I couldn't breathe."

Which explained exactly what had happened in the shower. What kind of bastard got his kicks from hurting someone like Chloe? "Why didn't you tell someone or leave him?"

Her shoulders rose and fell. "I was convinced it was me. And our marriage was good in most other areas." Her eyes closed. "At least, I thought it was. And I felt trapped, like there was no escape."

Trapped. Just like he'd felt when locked in that closet as a child. Just like he felt now when any relationship started to go on for too long. And like Chloe, he'd never told anyone about what had happened...until Jason had asked about the padlock hanging open on the back door of his house. Locked doors still made him edgy, even today. Would it be the same for Chloe with sex?

He looked down into her eyes. "You don't have to do anything you don't want to do. Ever. Do you understand me?"

"I wanted to. That's just it. I wanted it to be good for you. I just...couldn't."

"Me being with you makes it good, Chloe. I get pleasure out of *your* pleasure."

He watched as she digested that piece of information. When her brows puckered, and she appeared doubtful, he leaned back against the wall with a sigh, carrying her with him. "When I do something that makes you whimper, when you return my kisses—when my touch makes you fall apart. *That's* what gives me pleasure."

"Really?"

"Really."

She scrubbed the back of her arm over her eyes. "I'm sorry. For taking off like that."

He gave a soft laugh. "You scared me."

She touched his face. "Can we try again?"

Was she serious? He'd already screwed up once. Didn't trust himself not to do so again in the heat of the moment.

She reached up, her thumb brushing across his lower lip. "Please, Brad. I need to erase the bad memories and replace them with good ones."

"Are you sure?"

"Yes."

He hesitated. He'd already told himself this was the end—that he was all wrong for this kind of thing—but her heartfelt words and the fact that his body was responding to her touch in a way that was impossible to hide made him rethink his decision. If he said he didn't want to, she'd know he was lying, and the rejection might damage her more than she already was.

Helping her up, he went and switched off the shower then picked up two towels. Slinging one around his waist, he used the second one to dry Chloe off, patting every inch of her body then sliding the soft towel under and over her right breast, the nipple tightening as he did so. He repeated the act on the other side and lingered there until she leaned into the friction, her eyes fluttering closed.

His body responded instantly, and he put his mouth to her ear. "*That's* what gets my motor running." He dropped the towel to the floor and scooped her up in his arms and carried her off to bed.

Chloe rolled over, her breathing ragged, while his senses were still firing like crazy.

Brad followed her, leaning on one elbow as he stared down at her flushed cheeks, the faint sheen of perspiration on her brow. He'd allowed her to find her own way this time, although it had nearly killed him, his body straining under the pressure of keeping still. The result had been well worth it.

He might never recover, in fact.

Experienced or not, she set him off the second she touched him.

And that mouth. Lord. He'd tried to draw her away before

she got too close, but she'd brushed his hands aside, insisting. The heat of it as it had closed over his flesh…

He shuddered. It was like nothing he'd ever felt in his life.

The graphic image flashed through his skull, and he swallowed hard as a part of his anatomy defied gravity and stirred back to life. So soon.

What the hell was she doing to him?

"You're a witch," he whispered, reaching to brush her hair from her forehead, needing the contact, wishing he could roll her on her back and start all over again. But he didn't want to scare her.

Not the way he was scaring himself.

He'd never minded the mirrors the former occupants had left over his bed. Until today. Seeing their entwined images reflected back at him had taken his normally icy control and shaved it down to nothing. He'd barely lasted until she'd climaxed.

Her lips curved and she caught his hand, carrying it to her chest where her heart beat strong and firm against his palm. "So it was okay?"

"More than okay. Much more."

That was another problem. The sex had been good. Really good. Which could create problems down the road. As a doctor, he was used to patients—pregnant though they might be—getting a little case of hero-worship when the team helped them right a troubled pregnancy.

Chloe had been stuck in a terrible marriage, with a man who'd selfishly used her and given nothing back. Hell, anyone would look better than what she'd had. And she'd had her first *man*-made orgasm less than a week ago. The last thing he needed was for her to become infatuated with him. Because he couldn't be locked into a relationship. He'd feel as trapped as she had with Travis—as trapped as he'd felt as a kid. Things could turn ugly really quickly if he wasn't careful.

He dropped onto his back and put his hands behind his head, not bothering to cover himself. His reflection stared back at him, his need still very much in evidence. Disgusted, he flicked his glance over a couple of inches and found Chloe's eyes on him as well. Great.

Those mirrors were being ripped down from that damned ceiling the first chance he got.

As if realizing something was wrong, Chloe's brow puckered. "You okay?"

"Peachy."

Her head twisted sideways, looking at the real him, rather than the image above them. "Brad?"

Her voice had gone from purring contentment to uncertainty.

He was damned if he did. Damned if he didn't.

Well, then, he might as well make sure he was as damned as possible.

He reached for her and hauled her on top of him. "I'm fine. Just wondering if you've had enough lessons for one night?"

As if he'd actually taught her anything. She had been the one who'd taught *him* a thing or two.

"Can you? I mean, aren't you...done?"

He slowly ground against her. "Does it feel like I'm done?"

She gave a soft laugh. "I had no idea it was even possible."

"Yeah, well, neither did I." He nuzzled the fragrant skin just below her chin. "Which is why I've decided you're a witch."

Chloe wiggled her body until she was positioned at just the right spot, then slowly took him inside her, the air hissing from his lungs as the impossible became entirely probable. And any argument he might have made vanished in a puff of smoke, leaving only him and Chloe...and the fiery need that threatened to consume him.

CHAPTER NINETEEN

THE SOUND OF a buzzer awoke her, along with Brad's muffled curse.

"What is it?" she asked, cracking her eyelids and trying to focus on the glowing numbers of the clock. Eight o'clock. On Saturday. Wow, it was hard to imagine a week had gone by since that fiasco in the shower. A week of sharing Brad's bed. If she squinted her eyes just right, she could almost pretend they were in a normal relationship.

"It's the interphone. It must be the doorman. I'll see what he wants."

Levering himself out of bed, he walked to the door, his naked butt the best kind of eye candy there was. Chloe propped herself up on her elbow to watch, all thoughts of sleep gone. A second or two out of the room, she heard a thump and then a strangled curse.

She smiled. Not quite as cheerful this morning as she'd thought he'd be. Well, she was in a happy mood today. She'd gotten word yesterday that her paperwork at the hospital had gone through. She was officially part of the Angel's team. She and Brad had gone out last night to celebrate. Then had come back to the apartment and had another celebration. A much more private one.

She felt like a child who's just gotten her first taste of chocolate and couldn't stop gobbling it up, even though she knew she was eventually going to pay for her greed. But Brad was an intensely passionate—and pretty much insatiable—lover. Which served her purposes to a T. She'd never thought she'd see soreness as a good thing. But this was a different kind of discomfort, one that served as a reminder of all the pleasure that had gone on before.

Brad appeared in the doorway. "Get dressed."

The barked order took her by surprise. "What?"

He was already rummaging in his dresser for some clean briefs and dragging them over his hips. "Your brother is on his way up."

"Jason?" Her mind went blank for an instant before she realized exactly what Brad was saying. "Oh, my God," she shrieked, leaping out of bed.

Scurrying around, trying to round up her clothes, she yanked on the nearest article she could find, her shirt. Then found her jeans.

"Chloe."

"What?" Her voice was sharp with panic as she shimmied into the garment.

His hands circled her upper arms as he looked down at her, his eyes dark. "You might want to rethink your top. Unless you want me to drag you back to bed while your brother waits in the living room."

"My…" She glanced down and realized that not only was her white T-shirt on backwards but her nipples were clearly visible through the thin fabric. A very unladylike word exited her mouth followed by more panicked flailing as she tore apart the bedclothes in search of her errant bra.

"Looking for this?"

She cut a glance his way and found the item dangling from a lean index finger, his lips curved in amusement. Worse, he was already dressed, looking immaculately groomed except for the dark stubble lining his face.

He also looked perfectly edible.

Snatching her undergarment with a glare meant to cut him in two, she ripped her T-shirt back over her head and jabbed her arms through the bra straps. Her hands were shaking and she couldn't get the thing hooked at the back. Brad came to the rescue, snapping it, then his hands curved around to cup her breasts.

"Stop it." The man really was overwhelming sometimes. How could he be so blasé?

He did as she asked, but his raised brows said he was just as cool as he seemed.

And that doorbell was going to ring at any second. She turned her shirt right side out and yanked it on.

What were they going to tell Jason?

Nothing. She was a big girl, she didn't owe him an explanation. But he and Brad were best friends. She didn't want to jeopardize that.

She dragged her hands through her hair. "How do I look?"

"You want the truth?"

Her glance went back to her chest. Nothing was sticking out that she could see. Both girls were belted in place. "Yes, I want the truth."

"You look like you spent all night in my bed."

Her eyes widened. "Oh, God. That's not good."

He put his hands on either side of her face and planted a hard kiss on her lips. "I disagree. It was very good."

"But my brother…"

"Isn't going to know what happened unless you tell him." He skimmed a finger across her cheek. "Or unless you keep blushing every time I look at you."

She closed her eyes and sucked down a few quick breaths.

The bell at the front door went off, and she grabbed Brad's arm to keep herself upright.

"Relax," he said. "It's going to be fine."

The trip to the front door felt like she was marching to her own funeral. "No blushing. No blushing. No blushing."

Brad gave her a quick look as he put his hand on the doorknob then he pulled open the door. There stood Jason, a bouquet of daisies propped in the crook of his arm.

"Sorry for the short notice. I had some business in the city and thought I'd check and see how Chloe is doing."

Chloe was *doing just fine. Until now.*

Brad glanced her way, and her cheeks tingled, a sure sign that blood was about to be pumped into them. Time for damage control.

"I'm fine." The tingle turned to warmth, and Jason's eyes narrowed.

"Has Travis been bothering you? Because Mom and Dad warned him there would be repercussions—"

"No, he hasn't." *Let's just change this subject, shall we?* "But I am thinking about staying in the city on a permanent basis."

"What? The folks think you should come home. Stay with them for a while."

Brad spoke up for the first time, his voice smooth and sure. "The hospital has offered her a job. I think she's old enough to decide what she wants to do."

She was certainly old enough to share Brad's bed. Something she prayed Jason didn't figure out.

Her brother looked from one to the other before his gaze settled back on Chloe. "Where are you going to live?"

You mean once my lessons end and I'm declared frost-free?

"She can stay with me until she finds a place. I have a guest room."

Heat bloomed in her cheeks. That guest bed hadn't been used in a week.

Brad caught her eye, and one corner of his mouth lifted.

Yep. Her face was as red as the business end of a branding iron. And her handsome host had marked her for life.

"Let me just find something to put the flowers in. Thank you for bringing them."

"You're welcome."

Taking the flowers and feeling guilty for abandoning Brad, she hurried away to the kitchen.

Jason's voice, low as it might be, followed her into the room. "I'm holding you to that promise."

What promise? He had to be talking to Brad, not her.

"I haven't forgotten."

"Good. Because she's already been hurt by one asshole. Don't make it two." Her brother gave a quick laugh that was halfway between jest and warning. "Because I'll be coming for you if you do."

Jason had underestimated his sister.

Brad was rapidly discovering just how strong Chloe was. She was a great nurse, compassionate, efficient and capable as hell. Even if he hadn't had an ulterior motive in hiring her, she'd be a great catch for any hospital. Or for any man.

Anyone except for him.

As if summoned, she came out of one of the exam rooms, a file folder in her hand. She gave him a little wave and a smile.

Was it his imagination, or was there a little bounce to her step that hadn't been there two weeks ago?

Maybe there was. But that sexy little blush was still there, as strong as ever. All she had to do was look at him and her face lit up like a set of red Christmas lights.

He was almost sure that Layla had figured something out. And maybe even Cade.

That, on the other hand, gave him no pleasure at all. He'd made a huge mistake with Katrina and had paid dearly for it. He thought he'd learned his lesson, but maybe not.

But this wasn't a real affair, right? Emotions weren't involved. Not that they'd been involved with Katrina either. At least, not on his side. Sex was sex, and nothing more.

There were times he wondered if his parents had messed him up for good. Left him with a hole where his heart should be. Deprive a kid of love for long enough, lock him away where he can't be seen or get into trouble, and maybe that organ shriveled down to a useless hunk of flesh, good for nothing except pumping blood from one place to the next.

Chloe plunked the file into a holder outside one of the rooms and made her way over to him, bumping her shoulder against his arm. "How's it going?"

The playful tone seemed to heighten his recent misgivings. His lips tightened. "Let's keep our personal and professional lives separate, shall we?"

He knew he'd hurt her the second she took a step back, her teeth nibbling on her lower lip. "Sorry. No one's around, and I just thought..." She squared her shoulders. "It won't happen again."

Jason's words came back to haunt him: *"She's already been hurt by one asshole. Don't make it two."*

"Hey." He reached for her hand, only to have her take another step back.

"I have to get back to my patient, Dr. Davis." The cool tone and her use of his title drilled home the fact that he couldn't hold her to one standard while holding himself to another. In other words, hands off while at the hospital. It seemed to have worked a little too well, because her cheeks weren't pink at the moment, they were as pale as ivory. She wasn't thinking about the way they'd passed their morning before coming to work.

And he doubted he'd be passing his evening that way either.

Aware of Brad's eyes following her progress, she headed for the exam room. She knew he wanted to keep things quiet at work, so why had she gone and done something so stupid? Because it was hard for her to compartmentalize things the way Brad evidently could. He could make love to her by night and then coolly go about his day as if nothing had happened.

And really it hadn't. Not for him anyway.

Just as she touched the door, the phone at the nurses' station buzzed.

Damn. So much for a quick exit. Ignoring him and moving back to the central desk, she picked up the phone. "Prenatal, this is Chloe."

"Hey, Chloe. Guess who?"

The blood drained from her face at the sound of the voice on the other end of the line. "Travis?"

Out of the corner of her eye she saw Brad's head swivel her way. She put her head down and stared at an open chart, hoping he'd just go away. Why did the men in her life have to end up being jerks? Although somehow Brad's words had wounded her much more than Travis's ever had. Something she didn't want to dissect at the moment. "Why are you calling me?"

"Why do you think? I made a mistake. I want you to come home."

This time, rather than the show of tears he'd put on the last time he'd gotten caught, there was an almost sneering quality to his voice that made her skin crawl. As if he knew something she didn't. "You can talk to my lawyer. We're through."

Hopefully Brad had already gone off to see a patient or something.

"Not quite. Did you know your parents pulled their accounts last week?"

What did that have to do with her? "Does that surprise you? It would be kind of a conflict of interest to manage your ex's parents' investment funds, don't you think?"

"No, because we're going to kiss and make up."

She couldn't believe he'd actually said that. "That's not going to happen."

"No? I'm sure they…and your lawyer would be interested in knowing that you're now shacking up with your boss. Along with other more interesting things."

Was he threatening her? How did he even know about Brad? She glanced up to find the man in question standing in front of the desk, brows lifted in question. She shook her head and motioned for him to go away. He stayed right where he was.

"Good luck with that," she said. "If you think my parents are going to be railroaded into letting you handle their financial affairs, you're sadly mistaken."

"It might be fun to try. How's that working out, by the way? Is he tired of playing doctor with a terminal patient yet?"

Meaning her. Oh, God. And she'd thought he couldn't hurt her any more. She should have hung up the second she'd heard his voice. Why hadn't she? Because she'd wanted to make sure he didn't hurt anyone else she cared about.

Tears formed in her eyes and she averted her glance, terrified she might break down in front of Brad. He'd already witnessed one freak-out session, she didn't want to make it two. "He…he isn't playing doctor—"

Fingers prised hers from the receiver, making her realize just how hard she'd been gripping it. Putting the phone to his ear for a second or two, Brad listened before dropping it back onto the handset.

"I'll have his calls blocked."

She twined her hands together, bile rising in her throat. "He threatened to tell my parents about us."

"Let him."

She blinked back her surprise. How could he be so calm about it after he'd lectured her earlier for teasing him? It brought to mind what she'd heard her brother say the other morning. "Did you promise Jason you wouldn't sleep with me?"

"I did." He didn't bat an eye.

"Then why did you?"

"I didn't want you sleeping with someone else to get what you need."

She nodded. Her voice small, she had to ask the question that had hovered since their first time together. "Did you want me at all?"

He reached over to finger a strand of hair that had come loose from her ponytail. "I think I've already answered that question as well. Do you want me to prove it right here?"

Something in her relaxed. Travis knew exactly where to hit her, but Brad knew exactly how to calm her fears. She was almost ready to forgive him for his earlier words. "What about keeping the private and professional lives separate?"

"I shouldn't have said that, Chloe. I know you're not going to broadcast it over the hospital loudspeaker."

She thought about Travis's call. "I don't need to, evidently."

"You want to know what I think?"

Did she? Maybe he thought they should call a halt to things. "Yes."

"He was fishing. He doesn't know anything."

He paused, his hands dropping to his sides before he continued. "That man damaged something very precious, and I'll never forgive him for that."

Chloe swallowed back a wave of emotion. This coming from Brad—a man who, as a boy, had been dealt a hand just as bad as hers. Worse really, because she'd made a conscious decision to marry Travis, whereas Brad hadn't had a say in who had raised him. "I feel the same way about your parents. I hate what they did to you."

He stiffened, his face clearing of all emotion. Before he could respond, though, Ginny came round the corner and sat at the desk. Brad nodded at the other nurse and then asked for updates on a couple of patients, casually thumbing through the files in question.

How could he flip the switch on his emotions like that?

A few seconds later he said he had a meeting to attend and walked away. As he waited for an elevator, Chloe got this weird sinking feeling in the pit of her stomach that grew as he stepped into one, the doors sliding shut and hiding him from view.

Someday they would be doing this for the very last time. Either Brad would move on or she would, and this part of their relationship would be over for ever. And as much as she hoped otherwise, she didn't think they'd ever be able to go back to being just friends.

Because she loved him. And she had for a very long time.

CHAPTER TWENTY

"I JUST GOT word that your twin-to-twin transfusion patient is in labor." Layla's concerned voice met her as she came into the lobby.

"What?" Chloe's heart sank. Two weeks had gone by since the woman's surgery and things had looked so promising.

"They're trying to stop it, but it looks like they may be too late. They're giving her steroids, just in case."

To help the babies' lungs develop. At thirty weeks, the twins could survive, but not without some major intervention. And one or both babies could have deficits to overcome, especially the donor twin.

"Where is she?"

Layla put her arm around her shoulders. "She's up in Labor and Delivery."

That meant they didn't really expect to stop labor altogether, just delay the inevitable.

"Is Cade there with her?"

"I'm sure he must have been called in, as he did the surgery."

"Thanks. I think I'll go up and see how she's doing."

Layla gave her shoulders one more squeeze then let her go. "There's a team standing by to take over if she delivers."

"Where's Brad?"

"I haven't seen him in a while."

Neither had she. They'd gone their separate ways that morning after arriving. He said he'd see her back at the apartment, hinting that she'd need to take the subway home.

They'd made love last night, but had there been something a little more reserved about him than usual?

Probably her imagination. Not in her imagination was the horrifying realization that her teenage infatuation hadn't dried up after all. It had lain dormant in her subconscious—like a seed—waiting for a drop of water to make it spring back to life.

Well, it had gotten not just a drop, not just a trickle, but a whole waterfall over the last couple of weeks and, like the beanstalk from the fairy tale, had grown to terrifying proportions.

Only it wasn't infatuation. It was love. And although she couldn't exactly pinpoint when it had started, she remembered the deep fear she'd felt when Brad had walked through the door to her family home after his motorcycle accident. Limping. Bleeding. Hopelessness in his eyes that had shocked and frightened her.

Jason's words about the locks in Brad's house had sprung to mind. About how cruel someone would have to be to do that to a young, vulnerable child. And she'd hated his parents with a fury that had never completely died.

And neither had her feelings for him, evidently. She'd felt the warning signs when she'd danced with him at the wedding… and when he'd asked her to go for a ride on his bike after he'd graduated from medical school, but she'd refused.

What if he'd suddenly realized how she felt and was upset about it? She'd been careful to keep her emotions in check last night as he'd brought her to fulfillment, biting her lips to avoid saying or doing anything that might tip him off.

But maybe he'd seen through her act and was trying to figure out a way to let her down easily.

Well, that was impossible. If she'd thought her heart had

been broken over Travis, she had no idea how it was going to survive the tidal wave of hurt now bearing down on it.

And Brad didn't have to do anything to make it happen. This time, it was all her.

Brad had cured her of one problem, only to be the cause of another. Much in the way that radiation could cure one type of cancer while causing another type to develop further down the road.

She sighed. And how was that for an insensitive comparison? Her problems were mild compared to what her twin-to-twin patient was going through right now. Better to focus her energies on praying for those babies' survival rather than rail at the fates over something inconsequential. Because, ultimately, she would survive this.

The maternity wing was a beehive of activity with groups of doctors and nurses discussing cases, while behind one of those doors lay Clara Serrano, fighting for her children's lives.

Surprisingly, she spied Brad in one of the clusters—the same one that Cade was in. She didn't think he'd be here, and the fact that he'd not even tried to find her to tell her about Clara made her insides cramp.

She'd come up to see what was going on, but hesitated, feeling very much like an outsider all of a sudden. Brad glanced up from his discussion and saw her, and motioned her over. Again she hesitated. If he'd wanted her here, he would have called her like he had the day Clara had had her surgery. Instead, her cellphone had remained silent as she'd drunk her coffee alone in the park.

Alone. Maybe that's what she was meant to be.

When she started to back toward the elevators, Brad broke away from his group and came towards her. "Were you looking for me?"

She shook her head. "I heard Clara had been admitted and

came to see how she was doing." Another flare of hurt erupted. "Why didn't you call me?"

"I didn't realize you'd want me to." There was a cool edge to his voice she didn't like.

"She was one of my patients."

He glanced away for a second before looking at her again. "There was nothing you could do. I didn't want to worry you."

There was more to it than that but, other than call him a liar, what could she do?

The urge to spin away and get back into the elevator was almost overwhelming, but she forced her feet to remain where they were. Her chin went up. "I thought we'd already established that I'm a big girl. I can take care of myself."

He studied her face before nodding. "Come back over with me, then. You can get caught up on what's happening."

Chloe stood in the group and listened as various updates came from Clara's room.

"Contractions are still progressing, unfortunately. There's no going back now." The latest doctor to exit the room broke the news everyone had been dreading. "Let's get ready."

Clusters of people broke apart hurrying in various directions to do their parts in making sure mother and newborns had the best possible shot at a good outcome.

"Did the ablation procedure benefit the smaller twin at all?" she asked Brad.

"It's only been a couple of weeks so theoretically it had an effect, but it's hard to tell just how much of one at this point."

She nodded. "I have to get back to work. Will you let me know how it goes?"

"Sure."

He tweaked her ponytail as she turned to go, and when she glanced back over her shoulder, he was smiling. She sucked down a lungful of air, feeling the tension drain from her body. Maybe those weird vibes she'd been feeling had been the result of an overactive imagination. It wouldn't be the first time she'd driven herself crazy coming up with the worst possible scenario and then worrying it to death. Except in the case of her ex it had been all that and more.

She could only hope that this time she was wrong.

The next few hours passed in a whirlwind of activity for Brad. Word had gotten around the hospital about Clara Serrano's condition, and he'd been fielding all kinds of questions. He could only imagine what the phones were like in other parts of the hospital. The administrators must be buried under an avalanche. Laws prevented them giving out specifics on the patient, but because the syndrome was relatively rare, other facilities would soon be asking questions to help them deal with their own cases.

Clara still hadn't given birth, but they were expecting the babies to make an appearance at any time.

He hadn't seen Chloe again since their encounter on the floor of Labor and Delivery, but he hadn't gone out of his way to see her either. She'd acted differently last night, and although he couldn't put his finger on what it was, there'd been a sense of detachment that hadn't been there on previous nights.

Oh, she'd been just as sensual as always, but he couldn't shake the feeling that she'd been holding something back. That had bothered him. But what had stunned him even more had been his reaction to it. In his previous relationships, when one or both parties had begun to cool, he'd been fine with it. Had had no qualms about walking away. Anything was better than being locked into something with no way out.

This was different. He'd held onto Chloe just a little bit tighter, almost as if trying to pull her closer, even as he felt her emotional withdrawal. Why did he care so much? This was supposed to be a temporary arrangement. It *would* be a temporary arrangement.

He just had to convince his heart of that.

That was the tricky part. He'd been programmed from childhood that withdrawal was normal. That the more you cared about someone, the further away they would pull. And if you fought against it, tried to do something that got you noticed… the locks began clicking shut.

That was just the way it was. He'd learned his childhood lessons well and had the routine down to a science. Either he pulled back or the woman did. Either way, the result was the same. A relatively painless separation. And he remained free to move on.

Just because that wasn't how things worked in the Jenkins family it didn't mean that he should start smothering those around him or trying to hang onto something that was obviously not meant to be.

Like him and Chloe?

Exactly like that.

So why had she acted so wounded when he hadn't called her about Clara Serrano? He was just saving them both some heartache. If she wanted to fling open that door and walk away, he was going to let her—it wasn't locked. His gut churned at the thought.

Maybe it was harder for her to pull back because she'd been wired differently. Her childhood had been spent in the bosom of her family, protected and cared for. Was that why she'd been so quick to believe the rubbish Travis had dished out about a love that lasted for ever?

In his experience, it didn't. And if it did, he sure hadn't experienced it.

His gut twinged again, and he reached for a nearby bottle of antacids with a frown. All he needed right now was an ulcer.

No, all you need is Chloe.

Popping the pill into his mouth, he crunched down on it,

focusing on the sounds of his jaw pulverizing the pill, hoping it would obliterate that last thought as well.

He didn't need anyone.

The phone rang again. He swallowed and glanced at his watch as he picked up. Four-thirty. He'd be officially off duty in another hour. "Davis here."

"Bradley? This is your mother."

His eyes closed. Not today.

He couldn't remember her ever calling him at work before. Personal lives and professional lives had to be kept strictly apart.

Shock roiled through him as he realized he'd used almost those exact same words with Chloe the other day, explaining why she shouldn't tease him at work. The hurt on her face could have mirrored his own hurt each time his mother had aimed a well-manicured finger at the closet in his room.

Oh, hell, no!

"Bradley." His mother's voice was a little sharper this time.

"Yeah, I'm here."

"Aren't you going to ask me how I am?"

Was he? He should. It was social convention, and if nothing else, she followed that to a T. She expected him to follow suit. That's why he had a useless set of fancy dishes in his kitchen cabinets.

But it was easier to comply than to argue. "Of course. How are you, Mother?"

"I'm fine." Even though she'd been the one to demand he ask the question, she brushed it away just like she always did. He felt the muscles of his jaw stiffening, and he glowered at the bottle of antacids.

Before he could reach for them, she went on in her proper little voice, "Your father has received some distressing news."

His father. A nice enough man but one who'd never stood

up for his son, who'd let his wife discipline him however she saw fit.

"I'm sorry to hear that. Anything serious?"

"He has pancreatic cancer."

The words slipped by him almost without him noticing… until he pulled them back and paid attention. "Dad has cancer?"

"Yes. He found out a month ago." There was a slight pause. "He wants to see you."

A month ago. His father had cancer and no one had seen fit to call him until now. The acid levels in his stomach grew deeper, the antacid he'd just taken swept away in the onslaught. "Why?"

He was almost proud of the cool, indifferent tone of his voice, but inside a little boy cried out for a response. Wanted to know why his father hadn't loved him enough to intervene.

"He wants another opinion."

Ah, so that was it. This was no call for a sentimental re-union. His mother had a need for him, and she wasn't afraid to let her request be known. "I'm a prenatal doctor, Mom, not an oncologist."

"He still wants to see you. He has copies of all his tests and blood work."

He fought back a sigh. "I know an excellent doctor who specializes in—"

"Bradley!" His name cracked over the line. "If we had wanted another specialist we would have called one. He wants you."

Did she honestly expect him to drop everything and run to be by his father's side? He'd thought about trying to recon-cile with his parents over the years, but hadn't been sure he wanted to make the effort. And as they'd drifted further and further apart, the desire to settle things between them had drifted with it.

But if his father was already a month post-diagnosis, who

knew how much time he had left? If he didn't at least make the effort, could he forgive himself?

Probably not. It wasn't like they were on the other side of the world—just the other side of the state. He could be at their house in less than an hour. "I'm at work until Saturday. Will that be soon enough?"

"I'll tell him." There was no direct response to his question, so he assumed his father wasn't on his deathbed. A click on the other end confirmed that she'd hung up without saying goodbye.

Not that he'd expected it.

As he set the phone down, he stared at it, half expecting it to start jingling again. But it remained silent for once. And in the quiet of his office he tried to absorb the reality of his mother's words. His father had cancer and was asking for him.

CHAPTER TWENTY-ONE

BRAD WENT TO bed alone.

Chloe hadn't set foot in the guest room in two weeks, other than to get her clothes for the next day, so she was torn as to what she should do.

He hadn't said anything, but had come home looking drawn and sick. Before she could ask if he was all right, he'd disappeared into his room without a word and still hadn't re-emerged.

At nine o'clock she'd finally sat down and eaten a plate of leftovers for dinner, straightening the kitchen afterwards. It was now decision time. He'd said at the beginning of their arrangement that he wanted her in his bed every night, even when they weren't intimate. Did that still hold true? If not, wasn't she letting herself be used?

She drew her knees to her chest on the couch, knowing the answer to that was no. She was the one who'd asked for help, who'd practically flung herself into his arms. If he was tired of her, she had no one else to blame but herself.

And he had apologized for the incident in Labor and Delivery. Had said he didn't want her to worry. Things had seemed to be back to normal when she'd got in the elevator this afternoon.

So what had happened to change all that?

He hadn't even stopped long enough to tell her about the twins. Luckily, Layla had kept her abreast of the news as the afternoon had worn on. They'd been born, a tiny twin and an even tinier twin. But they were fighting with all their might. The next several days would give a more accurate picture of their prognosis. But at least they'd survived their birth. Each day was one step closer to health.

The door down the hallway opened, and Brad came down in sweat shorts and a T-shirt, a black and white sports bag clutched in one hand.

"Where are you going?" The question was ludicrous, but what else could she say?

"To the gym." He snatched the keys to his bike from the foyer table. "Don't wait up."

That was all very well and good, but it still didn't answer her question. Did she go to his room or not?

Not.

In his current mood she didn't think he'd be very happy to find her there on his return.

Fine. If he was okay with it, she would be too. She knew it was a lie, but maybe if she said it often enough, she'd eventually believe it.

Taking herself off to the bedroom, she shut the door a little louder than necessary, but what the hell. There was no one home to hear it. Still, it gave her a certain sense of satisfaction.

She pulled her clothes off and changed into a nightgown. She'd gotten used to sleeping in the buff, because Brad said he liked feeling her bare skin against his, but it seemed strange to sleep naked if it was just her.

Pulling back the beige striped bedspread, she crawled under the covers and grabbed the remote to the television. She idly flipped through the channels, pausing at a nature show where the image of a lion taking down a gazelle flickered across the screen. The huge feline held its prey by the throat, cutting off its air supply and suffocating the poor creature.

Chloe gulped and switched the channel, trying not to see

any similarities with her current situation. An old black and white western was the only other option, but it was better than lying in bed in the dark and brooding about what was wrong with Brad. If things didn't change, though, she was moving out. The sooner the better.

Brad frowned. He'd heard voices when he'd first come through the door to the apartment and had assumed Chloe was on the phone. But the handset was in its holder. Maybe she was on her cell. He made his way back to his room, dumping the bag on the floor as he went through the door. His frown deepened. Chloe wasn't there.

Was he surprised? He'd barely spoken a word to her when he'd come home, but he hadn't been able to. If he had, she'd have started asking all kinds of questions. Questions he hadn't been ready to answer. He'd had second thoughts about going to see his father and had decided to head to the gym and work off some of his frustration. He hadn't wanted to touch Chloe in his current state of mind. But now that he was back, he wanted to pull her close and let her sweet scent lull him to sleep.

The voices continued until a scream followed by sobs came from the guest room.

Had Travis somehow gotten into the apartment?

He went to the door and tried the knob, only to find it locked. That damn key! Why had he ever given it to her? Sweat began to form on his upper lip. "Chloe?"

No answer, but the sobbing continued unabated. The locks weren't meant to keep intruders out—or wayward children in—just to keep someone from entering a room unannounced. He put a shoulder to the door and shoved hard. The lock gave way and the door burst open, just as he'd suspected it would.

A figure on the bed moved. Sat up. The crying continued, but it wasn't coming from that direction. He pivoted and saw the television set. Still on. A woman on the screen being held at gunpoint.

"Brad? What's wrong?"

The adrenalin still pumped through his system, his heart pounding from its effects. He dragged a shaky hand through his hair, trying to calm his chaotic thoughts as he turned back round. "I heard... I thought Travis had somehow gotten in."

She reached on the nightstand for something. One click and the television went off, throwing the room into darkness. "Sorry. I must have fallen asleep with it on."

He came over and sat on the edge of the bed. "Is there a reason you're in here rather than in there?" He nodded toward the hallway leading to his room.

"Well...you didn't seem very happy when you came home. I thought it was better this way."

"It's not. Sorry for not making that clear." He smoothed her hair off her cheeks. "I got some bad news today and wasn't sure how to deal with it."

"Anything you want to talk about?"

"Maybe tomorrow." His arm went round her back and held her against him, needing the contact more than he should. "Come to bed with me."

"Are you sure?"

He nodded. "I want you next to me."

"Crawl in here with me, then." Chloe pushed the covers down her legs.

Brad stood and stripped off his street clothes, glad he'd chosen to shower at the gym. But when he got in and slid his hands down her back, they were met with some kind of flocked fabric. "Do you have to wear this?" he whispered. "I want your skin under my hands."

She sat up. "Help me, then."

He helped her shed her nightclothes and then folded her close, pulling the bedding up around them. Chloe snuggled against him and a few seconds later kissed the base of his throat, her fingers coming up to touch his face.

Although he knew she'd found the moisture there—wasn't sure exactly when his vision had blurred—she didn't ask about it or try to talk. She just wrapped her arms around him and squeezed. He squeezed back, the roller-coaster of emotions he'd experienced during the day quieting before sliding to a halt.

Chloe had somehow made everything all right. And she'd done it without uttering a single word.

They didn't need a second opinion. His father was dying.

He slid the last report back in its folder. "I don't understand."

His father reclined on the bed, and although he'd always had the body of a runner, wiry with ropy muscles, his cheeks were more angular than Brad had ever seen them. His skin was sallow, the yellow signifying liver involvement.

Brad's mother wasn't in the house: his father had sent her out to get something.

"I needed to talk to you alone. Tell you how…sorry I am. For the things that went on when you were younger. I didn't stand up to your mother when I should have." He paused and then cleared his throat. "I know if I don't say it now, I might never get another chance. I'm proud of you, Brad. You've become a fine man."

A fine man. One who didn't like locked doors and who couldn't be in a relationship for longer than a couple of months.

Brad waited for the anger to rise up and swallow him, but it wasn't there. All he felt was regret. "I appreciate you saying that."

What else was there to say?

"You'll be around for your mother after I'm gone? Despite everything that happened, I know she loves you."

Was he serious? Brad was the last person his mother had

ever wanted around. He swallowed, not sure how to answer. "She'll be fine. She's a strong woman."

His father shook his head. "I know it seems that way, but we married right out of high school. She was pregnant with you at the time. She's never been alone—really alone—in her entire life. She needs to know someone will be there once I'm gone, even if she won't come out and say it herself."

Why was his father telling him all this?

Because he was the fall-back plan.

Even as the thought went through his head, he dismissed it as ridiculous. But was it? His mother and his father had always presented a united front to the world—she was the brick and he was the mortar. His mother would be lost without him, despite her garden parties and all her social acquaintances.

She'd be as lost as he had been as a child.

"She'll need you," his father repeated.

Chloe came to mind. She'd needed him too. Things hadn't worked out with Travis, and she'd come running to him. Had asked for his help when it came to flirting and the bedroom.

Had he been her fall-back plan as well?

Bile rose in his throat even as he swallowed in one hard movement, trying to make the ugly thoughts disappear.

"She doesn't want me, Dad. She never has." Brad wasn't sure if he was talking about his mother or about Chloe. But maybe it was one and the same. And this was a hell of a time to realize he loved the woman who was currently sharing his bed.

Damn her. Damn his mother.

His father reached out and grasped his hand. "It might not seem like she wants you right now, but she will."

"And you expect me to just…"

He couldn't bring himself to say the words. *And you expect me to just drop everything…to forget how she treated me— how you treated me—as a child?* Because, despite his apology, his dad didn't realize what a huge impact those things had

had on him… All his dad knew was that they'd provided him with every material thing he could possibly want or need. And more. They'd given him everything.

Except love. And a childhood free of fear.

He'd had to go elsewhere to find that. And he had, in the Jenkins family. And most recently in Chloe Jenkins's arms— Chloe, who had her own issues with fear.

His whole life was one big circle of irony, which now seemed to be closing in on him as surely as that closet from long ago. His parents hadn't wanted him. Until now.

And Chloe hadn't wanted him either—had ignored him from the second she'd said "I do" to Travis.

Until now.

CHAPTER TWENTY-TWO

When was making love *not* making love?

When it was sex.

Chloe lay curled on her side in a tight ball, her breathing still heavy and uneven, while Brad stared at the ceiling. She'd been lying right beside him, still caught up in the afterglow, when her eyes had happened to meet his in the mirror and had been shocked by the cold emptiness she saw there.

She'd had to roll over to block out the sight.

She might love him, but he did not return the sentiment.

God, she was such a fool.

He'd shocked her tonight by coming through the door and grabbing her off the sofa. Pressing her against the nearest wall, he'd propped his elbows on either side of her head and stared down at her for a long time. Just as suddenly he'd lowered his head and kissed her. The second they'd touched, it had been as if a bomb had gone off. He'd devoured her, using his lips, his tongue...his teeth, his body telling her in no uncertain terms that he'd wanted her. Badly. Couldn't wait to have her. She'd never seen him like that before.

She'd been thrilled. Ecstatic. Surely he felt the same way about her that she did about him.

There'd been none of the slow build-up that had always gone on between them. He'd shoved her scrubs and panties down and off and had lifted her onto his hips, burying himself inside her within seconds. Had carried her to bed like that. Still kissing. One hand under her butt, the other buried deep in her hair, holding her to him as he'd groaned into her mouth and surged inside her with each step.

Then she'd free-fallen onto the bed, with Brad still on top of her, still inside her. All around her.

She hadn't known what had been going on in his head, but whatever it was she'd been right there with him. Had been ready for him the second he'd touched her. She'd scratched and bitten and moaned out her need, her hips rising to meet each thrust. She'd tasted blood, but didn't know whose it was. His? Hers?

God!

She'd gone up in flames. Had held onto him as she'd come crashing back down to earth.

Until she'd realized he had no longer been holding her. Tension had radiated off him as he'd pulled out of her without a word, rolling onto his back. She'd frowned, glancing into the mirror above her.

And she'd seen it.

Lord, she'd almost told him she loved him, had gritted her teeth at the last second and let the words sing through her head instead. What a disaster that would have been, if she'd said them out loud.

He'd have laughed in her face.

Or worse.

She pulled in a careful breath as she lay there. Then another one, before she got up the courage to say the words. "Do you want me to leave?"

Chloe didn't know exactly what she meant by the question. Wasn't sure if she was talking about his bedroom or about his life.

The silence was deafening. Her heart gave a few painful

thumps. But when she braced herself to get up, his hand was on her hip, gripping tight. "No. Don't go."

"Are you sure?"

Brad rolled on his side and put his arm around her. "Yes." He pulled her back against him. "I'm sorry. Did I hurt you?"

She swallowed, tears burning at the back of her eyes as she realized what was wrong with him. That's why he'd looked that way. Why he'd been so stiff and unyielding. He thought their lovemaking had been too rough, that he'd hurt her like Travis had done.

"No. Couldn't you tell?"

His arm tightened. "I wasn't paying attention to anyone but..." a beat went by "...myself."

She turned her head and kissed his upper arm, where his tattoo was. "I got a little carried away too. I think I might have bitten your lip."

There was a pause as if he was testing out that admission. "I didn't even feel it."

Her cheek rubbed where her lips had kissed. "Didn't you feel anything?"

"I felt everything. Except that." His chest rose and fell in a sigh. "I don't want to hurt you, Chloe."

She stiffened. Was he still talking about the sex? "I already told you, you didn't. I'm fine."

"Are you?"

What was with the enigmatic questions? Just when she'd thought she had him figured out, he changed direction and confused her all over again.

She shifted in his arms, until she was facing him. She swept the hair off his forehead, like she'd done in the park. That day seemed like ages ago. "What's wrong, Brad?"

His throat moved. "My father has cancer."

Chloe stared at him. "My God. When did you find out?"

"A couple of days ago. I went to see him today."

And then he'd come home and taken her to bed. The desperation she'd sensed in him hadn't been because of her at all but because of the devastating news he'd gotten. It also explained the emotional withdrawal she'd sensed in him over the last couple of days.

"Is it serious?"

He nodded. "Terminal."

She grabbed his hand. "I'm so sorry. It's good that he wanted to see you, though."

"He wants me to take care of my mother."

Chloe searched his eyes, but they were devoid of emotion. "Take care of her how?"

A quick shrug. "He wants me to be there for her."

Now she understood. His father wanted him to be there for a mother who'd never been there for Brad. Not really. Her heart ached. "Will you?"

"I don't know. I'll have to give it some thought."

The coolness in his voice sent a chill over her, but she hadn't walked where Brad had walked. Hadn't been on the receiving end of abuse that drove you to despair, drove you to take chances you knew you shouldn't. She thought about Travis. Well, maybe she had walked a mile or two in his shoes.

Maybe more than that. Hadn't her experience with Travis caused her to look up an old friend and ask him to have sex with her? And then gone and stupidly fallen in love with him?

Oh, yeah. She'd taken some chances that she'd known she shouldn't. And had taken them anyway.

She pushed the thought away. It wasn't the same thing at all. *Wasn't it?*

Clearing her throat, she cast around for something to say. "How long does he have?"

"Three months. Maybe four."

Sadness washed over her. She would probably be out of

Brad's apartment by that time. Would he even tell her what was happening with his father?

Maybe. The lovemaking they'd just shared said he might.

And as much as she wanted to close her eyes and ignore it, a little kernel of hope was lodged firmly in her heart. Like a blood clot that preceded a heart attack?

God, she hoped not.

Maybe there was the equivalent of a clot-busting drug she could take that would get rid of the thing once and for all.

Or maybe she could just ignore whatever it was and pray she had the symptoms all wrong. That what she'd thought was love was actually just a bad case of indigestion that would soon wash through her system, never to be seen again.

Yeah. Right.

Because lying in bed with him right now, she knew there was no place she'd rather be. Now, if she could only convince Brad to give them a chance…

CHAPTER TWENTY-THREE

"Mom, how are you?"

Chloe opened the door to the apartment and gave her mother a hug. Her mother was earlier than she'd expected. Thank heavens Brad had already left for work and she was up and dressed. First Jason and now her mother. But at least her mother had called last night to make sure it was okay to drive over. No rushing around to cover up her and Brad's nocturnal activities.

"I know you said you were fine, but I wanted to come by and see for myself." She cupped her daughter's face and studied her. "You look good. Happy."

"I am. I feel like I've been given a new lease of life." She tugged her mother inside. "I have some coffee made if you want some. Can you stay? Oh, I have so much I want to tell you."

Her mom laughed. "There's a new-fangled device called the telephone, you know." Her smile faded. "I kept hoping you'd call. Jason said you were doing okay, but I was worried."

Chloe led the way into the kitchen and pulled down two tea cups. Brad's mother's china pattern. The woman he was supposed to take care of. "I'm doing better than I expected. I really like working at the hospital."

"And how's Brad?"

"Fine." She concentrated on pouring the hot liquid into the cups, hoping her cheeks weren't steaming as much as the coffee. "He wants me to stay in the city." She clarified, in case her mom got the wrong idea. "At the hospital."

"And what do you want to do?"

Chloe desperately wanted to believe in happy endings. Wanted to stay here. With Brad. And be a part of his world. But she didn't know if it was possible. He hadn't spoken about feelings per se or hinted that he wanted to deepen their relationship. "I think I need some time to figure things out."

"That makes sense." Her mom spooned some sugar into her cup and stirred. "It was good of him to let you stay."

"Yes." She poured milk into her own cup. "Let's go into the living room."

Chloe put a tray on the center ottoman and set her cup and saucer down. "How's Daddy?"

"He's helping put a new roof on the community center."

"In this heat?"

Her mom took a sip of her coffee. "You know him. Thinks he's still in his thirties."

"Yes, he does." How could one father be in the prime of his life at fifty and another father be dying? It didn't make sense. She couldn't imagine losing one of her parents…would be devastated when it happened.

But not Brad. Or maybe he'd just buried his feelings so deep no one could get to them. Not even the man himself.

Could she blame him? After the way his childhood had been?

But it wasn't just his parents he seemed to be apathetic about. He'd had dozens of women over the years, probably more. And yet none of them had made a dent in that armor he wrapped around himself. He'd never mentioned Katrina again. It was as if the woman had never existed.

As much as Brad disliked locks, that hadn't stopped him from boarding up his heart and padlocking it shut. Who knew if the right key even existed? Or if it did, if she could find it. She had no idea where to start looking.

Her mom was saying something, looking at her quizzically.

"I'm sorry, what?"

"I asked how you like the city so far."

That was an easy question. "I love it."

"I was kind of hoping you might want to come home. We miss you."

Chloe wrapped her hands around the delicate china cup, the expensive porcelain feeling brittle all of a sudden beneath her palms. "I miss you too. I just don't think I can go back right now."

"Maybe after the divorce goes through?"

"Maybe."

"Do you need me to stop by the house and pick up your clothes? Or I could ask Travis to send them."

The thought made her cringe. "No, I don't want anything that's there." Clothes and shoes were replaceable, and she'd rather not have any reminders of that time.

Her mom was silent for a moment or two. "What happened, Chloe?"

Lord, she didn't want to go through any of the sordid tale. "He hurt me."

"Physically?"

"He didn't hit me, no." She was going to leave it at that. No need to tell her family that what had started out as verbal ridicule had escalated into a form of abuse. Layla's words had convinced her it really had been. How far would he have gone if she hadn't found out about his affairs? Maybe he'd even wanted her to discover the truth just to hurt her more.

"I'm sorry, honey. Why didn't you come to your father or me?"

"I just couldn't." Maybe for the same reasons Brad had never told anyone about his own abuse.

"Chloe, look at me."

Her eyes came up and found blue eyes so like her own probing, trying to find a way to help, just like she always had. Tears pricked and she blinked to keep them at bay.

Her mom took the cup from her hands and placed it on the tray, then she pulled Chloe close and wrapped her arms around her. Chloe rested her head on her shoulder, just like she had when she'd been a little girl, and let her mom's love wash over her. "Don't let anyone do that to you again." Another pause. "Not even Brad."

She tensed. Had her mom figured out what they were doing? Had she realized the depth of Chloe's feelings for him? Maybe. She was a smart woman. "I won't, Mom. I promise."

He missed her.

The thought kept pricking at him all day long at work, like a splinter he felt constantly but couldn't find and pull out. She was off duty, spending time with her mother. He didn't like the way her absence left a hole in him, but wasn't sure how to deal with it. Ever since he'd left his father's house he'd been feeling more and more uneasy about the way things were headed. Sooner or later the whole situation would start closing in on him, just like it always did. And by delaying the inevitable, they were both going to pay the price. Soon.

He might not be the smartest guy in the world, but he knew deep down he couldn't give her what she wanted—what she deserved—any more than Travis had. Maybe he could in the bedroom but not emotionally. He might love her, but he was smart enough to know he didn't do those kinds of feelings well. Chloe, on the other hand, embraced those soul-searing emotions, maybe a little too well. It's why she'd been so damaged at Travis's hand after their marriage. She'd trusted him and he'd betrayed that trust—in more ways than one.

Wasn't she leaving herself open to more hurt by getting involved with him? He dragged a hand through his hair as the splinter inside him pushed deeper, poking at places he'd rather not examine.

He and Chloe might be able to come together for a period

of time, but there was no way it could last long term. He didn't do relationships like the one Mr. and Mrs. Jenkins had. One that seemed to flourish for decades. Chloe's family had had room not only for their own children but for a lost soul who'd appeared on their doorstep beside Jason.

How did someone open their hearts like that? He had never been able to get to that point. He was really good at superficial relationships that didn't require anything more than a couple of nights a week. But every day? For the rest of his life? He didn't think he had it in him.

He suddenly understood the shaky panic that had closed in on Chloe as she'd knelt in the shower stall that day. The one that had caused her to wheel away and run. Because that's exactly what he wanted to do right now: run.

Chloe had claimed their time together would help prepare her for the future. Teach her how things worked in the bedroom. How men and women flirted and interacted in normal relationships.

Normal.

As if he could teach her anything about that. *Damn it!*

He should have left her to Coleman. No doubt the surgeon would do a hell of a lot better job than he could. Maybe he could even give her the kind of future she was looking for. Had this all been some kind of ego trip for himself? Some weird control thing…not wanting Chloe to be attracted to anyone but him?

The thought made his stomach turn over. Maybe he *was* as much of a destroyer as Travis had been.

Was it time to start backing off?

Maybe. Before things got too messy. Before Chloe got in over her head.

Like he was.

Chloe deserved the best that life could give her. And if she had to choose between him and Cade Coleman, using the eeny, meeny, miny, mo method, Brad was *not* it.

CHAPTER TWENTY-FOUR

"CLARA SERRANO'S TWINS are still hanging in there." Happiness bubbled through Chloe as she caught at Brad's hand in the empty elevator.

She'd stepped into it at the last second after she'd seen him round the corner and press the button. She hadn't seen him since that morning, and she wanted to talk to him. To see if that kernel of hope had any soil to cling to.

"I heard." He answered her statement by crossing his arms over his chest in a way that forced her to let go of his hand. He stared straight ahead.

She frowned. "Is something wrong?"

"No." His voice was calm, but even so...

Was he going back to the whole not mixing personal and professional stuff? She'd thought they'd already worked through that. "There's no one else in the elevator."

Brad nodded at the small camera mounted in the corner.

So he was worried. It wasn't like that image was broadcast to the whole hospital or anything.

They reached the ground floor, and the elevator doors opened. Brad waited for her to get out then followed her. "I'm going to be working late for the next several nights, so don't wait up."

The words sent a warning through her head that she chose to ignore. "Anything I can help with?"

"No, I just have to catch up on some things."

She blinked. Not much of an explanation. Something came to her. "Is it your father?"

"No. Just hospital business." He glanced to the left as if impatient to get away.

Chloe swallowed, trying not to see things that weren't there. Brad was not Travis. Working late did not mean the same thing it had in her marriage.

Except she and Brad weren't married. They'd never made any vows, hadn't promised to be faithful to each other for ever. Only for as long as their time together lasted. Maybe he was ready for it to be over and was hoping she could take a hint.

"I've got a meeting in a few minutes. Can you make it back to the apartment on your own?"

Her lungs burned as she tried to draw a slow, careful breath. "Yes. I'll be fine."

As he nodded and walked quickly down the nearest corridor, Chloe wondered if she really would be.

Over the next several days a troubling pattern emerged. Brad came home late at night and left before she got up in the mornings. She suspected he might even be sleeping on the sofa in his office and coming home just to shower and change clothes. She saw him in passing on the fourth floor, but he always seemed to be headed in the opposite direction.

A chill went through her, and it didn't take a brain surgeon to figure out he was avoiding her. She was back to sleeping in the guest room, and this time there was never a knock on the door. Never a hint that he wanted that to change. Thinking back to the last time they'd made love, despite the urgency she'd sensed in him, she couldn't help but wonder if he'd planned on that being their last time together. Her treatment had run its course, and he was ready to move on to the next patient.

Shuffling some papers at the nurses' station, she jumped

when Ginny's voice came from her left. "You okay, honey? You're looking a little pale today."

The nurse sat in the seat next to hers. Chloe wasn't sure what to say. Talking to her about Brad was out of the question. But she was going to have to make a decision because she couldn't go on like this.

"I'm fine." Chloe closed her eyes for a second or two. "No, I'm not, actually. I need to get some fresh air. Can you cover for a few minutes?"

Ginny glanced at her watch. "You're only a half-hour away from finishing your shift. Why don't you go on home?"

"Thanks. I think I will." Impulsively, she leaned over and gave the other woman a hug. "You've been incredibly nice to me. Thank you."

"Hey, it's not like you're going away for ever. Are you working tomorrow?"

"No, it's my day off." Her mind tried not to look more deeply at Ginny's words. *It's not like you're going away for ever.*

"Go home and get some rest, then. I'll let Brad know."

As if he'd care. She should probably hunt him down and demand to know what was wrong, but deep in her heart she already knew. Asking for verification—or, worse, begging him to change his mind—would just make her seem needy and desperate. Just like she'd been when she'd gone to Travis's hotel room.

She rode the elevator to the ground floor and made her way into the heat of the afternoon. The park across the street beckoned to her and she headed for it, glancing at the bench where she'd drunk coffee several times. The air was warm and muggy but she needed to think before getting on that subway and riding home to Brad's empty apartment.

As she wandered down the nearest path, trying to figure out what was going on with her...and with Brad, her mother's words came back to her, whispering a plea that she couldn't ignore. *"Don't let anyone do that to you again. Not even Brad."*

That wasn't what forced her to a decision, though, it was her response to her mother's statement that did. "I won't. I promise."

If she stayed here one more day, she'd be breaking that promise.

Her eyes filled with tears but she stood up straighter and pulled in a long deep breath. She may have been like an ostrich for the last few days, but she'd just lifted her head and taken a good look around. She was finally ready to take the hint. And as much as she didn't want to go back to Connecticut, that's where her family was. Not here in New York.

She'd allowed one man to pummel her heart into the ground. That was not a mistake she was going to repeat with anyone else.

Not even Brad.

Sitting on a nearby bench, she rummaged around in her purse for a pen and a piece of paper. Then with a sick heart and dry eyes she began to write.

Brad dropped into his office chair and scrubbed an exhausted hand across his face. He couldn't go on like this for ever without it eventually affecting his patients. He was going to have to face the music and do the deed. He'd broken things off with women before and, though it was never fun, it was always followed by a sense of relief. Certainty that he'd done the right thing.

So why couldn't he dredge up that certainty now?

Because he'd never loved any of the other women he'd dated.

Dragging in a breath, he decided to go home early. Chloe could stay with him until she found another place to live. He had some contacts in the city...so why hadn't he used them before now?

Because deep down he didn't want her to leave. But he knew that was what was best for both of them.

Reaching for his phone, he stopped short when he spied an envelope lying in the center of his desk…addressed to him. It was a hospital billing envelope so it wouldn't ordinarily raise an alarm, except for the neat, dainty letters printed in blue ink on the front of it. A stream of foreboding slid up his spine.

He planted his hand on the offending object and dragged it towards him.

Don't open it.

Ignoring his subconscious, he turned the envelope over and started to reach for his letter opener before he saw there was no need. The flap wasn't sealed. It was loose, allowing a peek at the sheet of paper inside. Pink. Feminine.

The foreboding grew.

Katrina had left an envelope very much like this one. But all he'd felt then had been irritation that she'd left him in the lurch.

The urge to pick up his phone and get hold of his doorman was strong—he could ask him to make sure Chloe didn't leave the building before he got home. But he didn't. Instead, he sat there for several moments, staring at that sheet of paper, the slight ticking of his black office clock keeping time with his thudding heart.

Well, hell. Sitting here wasn't going to change anything. He slid the paper from the envelope and opened it. When he'd finished reading, his hand slowly turned into a fist, crushing the paper, along with all his hopes and dreams.

She'd beaten him to the punch. He should be glad she'd let him off the hook. No hard talks. No trying to let her down easily.

But way down inside him was a deep-seated emptiness that no one would ever be able to fill again.

Because Chloe was gone.

CHAPTER TWENTY-FIVE

"I WARNED YOU not to hurt her."

Almost before Brad could register Jason's presence in his doorway, a fist connected with his jaw hard enough to send stars shooting across his field of vision.

When he could focus again, he saw his friend shaking his hand, swearing a blue streak. "Damn you, Davis. What the hell is wrong with you?"

Brad's jaw throbbed, pain coming and going in waves, but it didn't hold a candle to the agony he'd endured over the last couple of days. "Is that all you've got, Jason? Because I've beaten myself up a whole lot harder than that."

Pushing past him, his friend headed for the freezer and laid his hand across the nearest frozen item he could find. "I think I broke my damn hand."

"There are worse things to break."

Jason sent him a glare and then frowned. "You look like hell."

"Yeah? Well, a right hook'll do that to you."

"That's not what I mean and you know it."

Brad tested his jaw and winced, before walking over to his friend. "Let me take a look at that hand."

The door to the freezer slammed shut with enough force to send a gust of cold air rushing past his cheek, but Jason obediently held out his hand.

The purpling metacarpal of the middle finger caught Brad's attention, and when he pressed near the neck of the bone, his friend hissed a breath in. "God, what the hell did you do to my hand?"

"What did *I* do to it?" He tried a smile and then stopped as pain radiated through his jaw. "You're not going to be using this for a while."

"Too bad, because I'd planned on flipping you off on my way out of town."

His friend had every reason to be angry. Brad knew he should have called a halt long before things had gone as far as they had, but old habits died hard. He set Jason's hand on the bar and grabbed a bag of frozen peas from the freezer. Peas that Chloe must have bought because his freezer had been empty before she'd arrived. Just like his heart.

"Here. Hold this on it while I get my keys and take you to the hospital."

By the time Brad came back, Jason had parked his butt on the bar stool. "I can't ride on your bike with my hand like this. Besides, we're not going anywhere until you tell me what's going on. My sister won't talk to anyone, but we all know something's wrong. Something to do with you."

She hadn't told them? Not that he'd expected her to blurt out every unpleasant detail but he'd figured she'd tell her parents he'd treated her badly and that she'd had enough. He'd never actually expected her to leave the city, though. She'd talked about not wanting to go back to Connecticut until the divorce was final. The fact that she'd gone anyway made him wonder how deeply he'd hurt her. Jason's arrival added to that worry, driving salt into an already open wound.

He wasn't about to stand here and tell his friend he'd been sleeping with his sister, although Jason had probably already figured it out. Why else would he have let fly with his fists the second he had opened the door? "I wasn't trying to hurt her. I was trying to keep her from getting hurt."

"Yeah? Well, you didn't do a very good job. She's barely eating, just stares out the window. Dad thinks it's because of Travis." Jason adjusted the impromptu icepack, swearing again. "But I know the real reason."

Brad swallowed. Yep. Jason knew. "And what's that?"

"She's in love. With you. Although I have no idea why."

Hell. God, no.

This was what he'd been hoping to avoid. Why he'd pulled away. He tried to say something but the words caught in his throat. Stuck there.

Jason frowned, his eyes narrowing as he took a closer look at Brad's face. "Oh, man. It's not just her, is it? You love her back, don't you?"

"No, I…" This was his friend. Someone he trusted. He owed it to him to play it straight. "Yes. But I don't do long-term relationships, you know that. My folks—"

"Give that garbage a rest, Davis. How long have we been friends?"

"What does that have to do with anything?"

"Just answer the question."

Brad thought back. "I don't know. Twenty years. Maybe more."

"Exactly. That's pretty 'long term,' if you ask me." His friend smirked. "How many meals have you eaten at our house? How many ugly pairs of socks has my mom knitted you for Christmas?"

A smile came to his lips. "A lot. I still have most of those socks stuffed in a drawer somewhere."

"Bingo."

Something akin to hope blossomed in his chest. Was Jason right? They'd been friends for most of their lives. Jason knew him almost as well as he knew himself.

Could he be right about Chloe?

His history with her went back just about as far. When he'd graduated from medical school, she'd been the one he'd come home to celebrate with. But that wasn't all. The look of horror on her face the day he'd wrecked his bike had changed something inside him. His chest went tight as comprehension washed through him.

She saved you. Kept you from attempting anything else.

Memory after memory swirled through his head. Chloe in her wedding dress, blushing as she'd danced with him. On the back of his bike as they'd ridden to the hospital, her arms around his waist. Lying on a blanket in the park, her lips parting as she welcomed his kiss. Her gentle touch as she'd traced the lines of his tattoo. Gasping out his name as they'd made love.

He put the pieces of the puzzle together one by one. And the realization that came with it almost brought him to his knees.

He may not have learned how to love from his folks, but he had from his friends.

From Chloe.

He looked across the bar at Jason. "You're right. I love her."

"Now you're talking"

"Let's take you to get some X-rays. Then I'm going home." When Jason's brows drew together, he clarified. "Home to Connecticut."

"Come out of there, you little bastard."

Chloe wasn't sure if she was talking to the weed in front of her or the persistent pain in her heart, but she grabbed the plant with two hands anyway and tugged. It still wouldn't budge. With her headphones blaring a country tune in her ears, she grunted and repeated the act, only to have the plant slip from her grasp, sending her right onto her backside.

She swore again. Time to pull out the big guns. Reaching

behind her, she felt for her gardening shovel. If she couldn't pull the sucker out, she'd dig it up by the roots. Just like she was going to do with her wayward emotions. Her fingers closed over the handle of the shovel just as something shiny dropped onto the ground next to her hip.

She blinked, letting go of the shovel to push up the brim of her ball cap so she could see what it was.

It was a gold-colored key that looked like it came out of…

Her heart started tripping over itself as she turned and found a pair of boots standing behind her. Black leather. Attached was a familiar set of legs, narrow waist…leather motorcycle jacket.

"Brad." His name came out as a whisper of sound, the music in her ears all but forgotten. Until his lips moved and she realized she couldn't hear him.

He frowned, tilted his head and then squatted next to her, plucking one earbud from her ear and then the other. The music fell away.

Picking up the key, he reached for her hand then placed the object in her palm. She stared at it.

"I need your help opening something," he said.

She pushed air across her vocal cords, but nothing came out. She licked her lips and tried again. "Opening what?"

He rolled his fingers into a fist and pressed it against the left side of his chest.

Surely he couldn't mean…

"I don't understand. You wanted me to leave. You all but screamed it."

She noticed a dark smudge on the left side of his jaw.

"I know it seemed that way, Chloe, and I'm sorry. I had some stuff to work through."

"About your father?"

"No. About you and me." He touched the metal object in her palm. "I know I've done some stupid things and I'm not sure how to make them right. But no one else will ever hold that key. Only you. I'm asking you to use it."

She had to know for sure. No more guessing. "Use it on what?"

"Me."

Something in his voice made her take a closer look at him. "What happened to your face?"

A slow smile curved his mouth. "Would you believe that Cupid uses his fist nowadays instead of arrows?"

Cupid? Did that mean…?

As if he'd read her thoughts, he nodded. "I love you. I wasn't convinced I had what it takes to make you happy. I'm hoping I'm wrong about that."

Her fingers closed around the key. "You love me?"

"Yes."

One word. So very simple. And yet she heard Brad's heart and soul in it.

"I love you too."

His hand slid to the back of her neck and drew her toward him, resting his forehead against hers. "God. I didn't dare hope…"

She put her knees on the ground and twined her arms around his neck. "Neither did I." She breathed in the musky scent of rich leather and all things Brad.

He leaned down and kissed her, the lightest touch, just like he'd done at the park. It didn't stay that way for long, though. Soon it had grown and bloomed into something that couldn't be contained.

When it ended, she was gasping for breath and wanting him to do it all over again. Instead, he stood up and held out his hand. "I asked you to take a victory lap with me once upon a time, and you refused. I'm hoping this time you'll say yes."

"Yes," she breathed. Glancing at the curb, where his motorcycle stood waiting—*her* helmet resting on the seat—she started to stand up and then paused and held out the key to him. "Could you hold this for a second? I need to do one last thing."

Turning back to the weed that she'd struggled to pull out, she wrapped her gloved hands around it one last time and pulled with all her might. She felt the root shift and then break free from whatever had been holding it back. Then it was gone. Just like the junk in both of their lives.

She tossed it to the ground then stood with a smile and took the key from him. "I'm ready for that victory lap now, and I'm hoping it will carry us all the way home."

EPILOGUE

"Surprise!"

The lights came on as soon as Chloe and Brad entered the house. He smiled, glancing at Chloe to see how she'd react. The whole Jenkins clan was gathered behind the long farm-style table he'd eaten many a meal at as a troubled teenager. Ben and Jan were smiling, arms around each other's waists. Jason—sans arm brace after six weeks—wiggled his middle finger to show it was all healed and ready for business.

A shaft of pride went through Brad's chest. This family had opened its arms to him long ago. He now knew they'd be open whenever he needed them.

"What is this?" Chloe asked, glancing up at him.

"I kind of spilled the beans about what I was going to do tonight. I'd have been in big trouble if you'd said no."

She looked at the glittering diamond he'd placed on her third finger. He'd forced himself to wait until her divorce was almost final before asking her to start a whole new life.

With him.

She wrapped her arms around him and held him tight. "No chance of my saying no."

Chloe's mother came over and kissed her daughter's cheek, whispering something that made her smile. Jan then stood on tiptoe and kissed his cheek as well. "Chloe's a very lucky woman."

"I'm the lucky one, Mrs. Jenkins."

Chloe burrowed closer with a sigh. He could hardly believe this smart, passionate woman had agreed to be his wife.

Ben clapped him on the back and held out his hand. "Welcome home, son."

A mist rose in front of Brad's eyes, and he blinked a time or two before shaking the elder Jenkins's hand. "I appreciate that, sir."

Brad's real father was still holding his own, his illness seeming to be the wake-up call he'd needed to continue working on his relationship with his son. There was still a way to go. His mother was another story, but Chloe's sweet spirit was making inroads there as well, surprisingly.

"Come on, people. This is supposed to be an engagement party." Jason plucked a strawberry from a platter of sliced fruit and dipped it into a fluffy white concoction. "Besides, you guys are over an hour late and I'm starving. Dad has ribs outside on the grill." He popped the fruit in his mouth and then picked up another piece.

Chloe's cheeks turned a delicious shade of pink, and Brad knew she was thinking about exactly why they'd been late. She mouthed, *"I love you."*

He slung an arm around her shoulders and pulled her close, catching sight of the gold key she wore on a slender chain around her neck—the same one he'd placed in her palm all those weeks ago. He picked it up and fingered it, his eyes meeting hers as a silent promise passed between them. A reminder that love was strong enough to unlock any door, as long as they did it together.

* * * * *

Mills & Boon® Hardback

May 2013

ROMANCE

A Rich Man's Whim	Lynne Graham
A Price Worth Paying?	Trish Morey
A Touch of Notoriety	Carole Mortimer
The Secret Casella Baby	Cathy Williams
Maid for Montero	Kim Lawrence
Captive in his Castle	Chantelle Shaw
Heir to a Dark Inheritance	Maisey Yates
A Legacy of Secrets	Carol Marinelli
Her Deal with the Devil	Nicola Marsh
One More Sleepless Night	Lucy King
A Father for Her Triplets	Susan Meier
The Matchmaker's Happy Ending	Shirley Jump
Second Chance with the Rebel	Cara Colter
First Comes Baby...	Michelle Douglas
Anything but Vanilla...	Liz Fielding
It was Only a Kiss	Joss Wood
Return of the Rebel Doctor	Joanna Neil
One Baby Step at a Time	Meredith Webber

MEDICAL

NYC Angels: Flirting with Danger	Tina Beckett
NYC Angels: Tempting Nurse Scarlet	Wendy S. Marcus
One Life Changing Moment	Lucy Clark
P.S. You're a Daddy!	Dianne Drake

0413 GEN STD HB

Mills & Boon® Large Print
May 2013

ROMANCE

Beholden to the Throne	Carol Marinelli
The Petrelli Heir	Kim Lawrence
Her Little White Lie	Maisey Yates
Her Shameful Secret	Susanna Carr
The Incorrigible Playboy	Emma Darcy
No Longer Forbidden?	Dani Collins
The Enigmatic Greek	Catherine George
The Heir's Proposal	Raye Morgan
The Soldier's Sweetheart	Soraya Lane
The Billionaire's Fair Lady	Barbara Wallace
A Bride for the Maverick Millionaire	Marion Lennox

HISTORICAL

Some Like to Shock	Carole Mortimer
Forbidden Jewel of India	Louise Allen
The Caged Countess	Joanna Fulford
Captive of the Border Lord	Blythe Gifford
Behind the Rake's Wicked Wager	Sarah Mallory

MEDICAL

Maybe This Christmas…?	Alison Roberts
A Doctor, A Fling & A Wedding Ring	Fiona McArthur
Dr Chandler's Sleeping Beauty	Melanie Milburne
Her Christmas Eve Diamond	Scarlet Wilson
Newborn Baby For Christmas	Fiona Lowe
The War Hero's Locked-Away Heart	Louisa George

Mills & Boon® Hardback

June 2013

ROMANCE

The Sheikh's Prize	Lynne Graham
Forgiven but not Forgotten?	Abby Green
His Final Bargain	Melanie Milburne
A Throne for the Taking	Kate Walker
Diamond in the Desert	Susan Stephens
A Greek Escape	Elizabeth Power
Princess in the Iron Mask	Victoria Parker
An Invitation to Sin	Sarah Morgan
Too Close for Comfort	Heidi Rice
The Right Mr Wrong	Natalie Anderson
The Making of a Princess	Teresa Carpenter
Marriage for Her Baby	Raye Morgan
The Man Behind the Pinstripes	Melissa McClone
Falling for the Rebel Falcon	Lucy Gordon
Secrets & Saris	Shoma Narayanan
The First Crush Is the Deepest	Nina Harrington
One Night She Would Never Forget	Amy Andrews
When the Cameras Stop Rolling...	Connie Cox

MEDICAL

NYC Angels: Making the Surgeon Smile	Lynne Marshall
NYC Angels: An Explosive Reunion	Alison Roberts
The Secret in His Heart	Caroline Anderson
The ER's Newest Dad	Janice Lynn

Mills & Boon® Large Print
June 2013

ROMANCE

Sold to the Enemy	Sarah Morgan
Uncovering the Silveri Secret	Melanie Milburne
Bartering Her Innocence	Trish Morey
Dealing Her Final Card	Jennie Lucas
In the Heat of the Spotlight	Kate Hewitt
No More Sweet Surrender	Caitlin Crews
Pride After Her Fall	Lucy Ellis
Her Rocky Mountain Protector	Patricia Thayer
The Billionaire's Baby SOS	Susan Meier
Baby out of the Blue	Rebecca Winters
Ballroom to Bride and Groom	Kate Hardy

HISTORICAL

Never Trust a Rake	Annie Burrows
Dicing with the Dangerous Lord	Margaret McPhee
Haunted by the Earl's Touch	Ann Lethbridge
The Last de Burgh	Deborah Simmons
A Daring Liaison	Gail Ranstrom

MEDICAL

From Christmas to Eternity	Caroline Anderson
Her Little Spanish Secret	Laura Iding
Christmas with Dr Delicious	Sue MacKay
One Night That Changed Everything	Tina Beckett
Christmas Where She Belongs	Meredith Webber
His Bride in Paradise	Joanna Neil